THEOLYN BROCK

Other Books by Theolyn Brock:

LAKE CITY: STORIES FROM A COUNTRY-ASS TOWN

Acknowledgements:

I would like to thank the following people for reading the early draft of this manuscript and for all their valuable feedback: Jacqueline Brock, Kay Carpenter, Elaine Brown, and Kevin Burleson-Webb.

Forewarning:

This is a novel about death row criminals sent to an island. Their language is raw and unfiltered. The author has allowed the characters their natural human expression through the use of broken English, swearing, curses, oaths, and slang. As such, this book is not for children.

For Palmyra

CHAPTER 1: Must-See TV

"This shit should be on prime-time television." Agent Bledsoe's black, beady eyes were transfixed on the enormous high-definition monitors lining the office walls. He was jacked up on his fourth K-Cup of Butter Toffee coffee. To keep from comfort eating, he repeatedly clicked his Parker stainless steel retractable pen and tried not to chew his fingernails, already bitten to the quick. The fat of the thick skin around the edge of his thumbnails had been gnawed off the previous day.

His colleague, Agent Branson, held no such compunction about oral fixations, and no wife to pick at his expanding waistline. Branson's freckled right hand deftly spidered across the conference table, flipped open the top of the orange, pink, and white Dunkin' Donuts box, seized the first powdery jelly donut in range, and brought the delicious goodness up to his mouth without ceremony or a napkin. Before tucking in he remarked, "I see the coconuts swaying in the palms. The Black Hawks must be hovering overhead."

According to the continual radio transmissions, Operation Island X was going according to plan. The chosen inmates hailed from the Communications Management Unit (CMU) and the Special Confinement Unit (SCU) at the Federal Penitentiary in Terre Haute, Indiana. After full-body scans and head-to-toe physical inspections, a US Navy SEAL team (by special request) transported the shackled prisoners, who had been temporarily held in a California federal prison, to the remote tropical speck known only as Island X. The aircraft landed in Hawaii to refuel and again on an aircraft carrier in the Pacific Ocean. Since there was no place suitable for setting down on Island X, all the SEALs had left to do was drop the prisoners and return to Hickam Field.

"Where's Jessica?" Bledsoe asked. "You'd think she'd want to view this with us in real time."

"Probably putting out a fire." Branson shrugged, rolling his eyes. "Look!"

Turning back toward the monitor, Bledsoe gave an over-caffeinated jump, at which Branson laughed, when inmate Roderick Cooper struck the sand. The drone's camera zoomed in so close it was like Rod landed in their claustrophobic Washington field office and not almost 6,000 miles away on a sunny beach. As the canopy of Rod's parachute slowly descended and flopped over his head, Rod squealed in alarmed protest and curled into the fetal position. Obviously, the drone's speakers transmitting back to the field office were also functioning properly. As "Hot Rod," a schizophrenic, was easily the most nervous of the prisoners, it was predetermined to heavily medicate and shove him out first to avoid unnecessary tension with the other inmates.

Agents Bledsoe and Branson sat on pins and needles as the cannibal, Hans Fritzl—all 6'2" of him, still blonde and Aryan as a Hitler henchman at thirty-eight years of age—landed a good thirty feet away from Rod. Ignoring Rod, Hans didn't slow his roll. He grabbed the deflating billows of his parachute in a frenzy, scrabbled in the sand for a duffel bag, and ran, lumbering with his hands and arms full, into the dark brush with a knapsack bouncing on his lower back.

"Run, cannibal, run!" Bledsoe snorted at the monitors. "It figures…"

The third inmate, Trent Doyle, the bank robber, just barely missed the ocean when he hit the shoreline. Another drone zoomed in to capture his fall. The cacophony of his hooting emitted from the speakers in the Washington office.

Bledsoe kept a running commentary, clicking his pen and licking his full lips. "The SEAL team is tight. It's amazing how they are managing to get these wild turkeys safely on land, isn't it? Nobody's swimming or impaled on a tree."

"Speaking of which, I could use a shot of Wild Turkey," Branson replied.

Montgomery Davenport's landing was the most practiced of the bunch. At one point, long ago in his privileged life, he'd parachuted out of his uncle's Cessna and even base jumped before it became popular. He crouched, rolled, then stood upright. After extricating himself from the gear, he hustled down the beach as the final two prisoners exited the craft hovering above. A second Black Hawk circled the island as protectively as a mother eagle.

"A hundred dollars says the old senator's good-looking nephew won't last two whole days,"

Agent Bledsoe wagered, tapping his pen on the table. "Two hundred if the cannibal starts feasting on him."

"No. Two hundred the cannibal will ruin the op by eating Hot Rod first, if he eats anyone," Branson counteroffered with a chuckle, wiping the raspberry jelly from the corner of his mouth. "Hot Rod's the weakest and liable to drive anyone mad. Look, he can't even make his way out of the parachute."

Rod's squirming, tossing and turning body filled one screen, rolling in the fabric, humping and kicking like a revivified mummy. Both agents burst into roars of laughter.

"That's just pitiful," Branson said.

"Screw *Survivor* or *The Hunger Games, this* is must-see television. Real life—you can't make it up." Bledsoe dabbed the corners of his eyes with the hem of his tailored shirt, which had JDB embroidered on one cuff. "I wish we could release this footage. Or pay-per-view. You know, Bob, this...hilarity makes up for the last two years of hassle. Jessica has been riding my ass like a cowboy with spurs. My wife says I'm never at home, and when I am home all I do is eat and sleep. But now we finally get to sit back, watch, and take notes. We'll probably never have to trigger a drone. Tell me again why we couldn't give Hot Rod a lifetime prescription of...what do they give him, Haldol?"

"He wouldn't take it anyway. You know that." Branson reached for another donut. "Whatever sedative they tranquilized him with for the journey must have worn off."

"High tolerance. Well, let the hallucinations begin. Boy, oh boy."

The gang member, Guerrero, landed in a squat and skidded, digging a long trench into the sand.

"He'll be digging sand out of his ass," Bledsoe said.

To the agents' further surprise, the kidnapper, Shane Lubbuck, landed flat on his back, which knocked the wind out of him. His was the clumsiest landing. Bledsoe and Branson held their collective breath, waiting to see if he was alive. Ganked on adrenaline, Lubbuck paused a few beats, gasped, arched his back, and hopped up with alacrity. Doyle, Guerrero, and Lubbuck gleefully jumped up and down, slapping each other's backs and high-fiving, spontaneously howling, hollering things like, "We're free! Out of our cages forever! Fuck yeah!" and punching the air with their fists.

Bledsoe winced. "Turn down the sound a little, Bob."

"You know this op is never going to see the light of day."

As the Black Hawks circled to leave, Lubbuck flipped them off with both hands held high in a hearty salute until the craft were nothing but disappearing dots in the sky.

"What an asshole," Bledsoe declared, shoving his empty coffee cup across the table.

"What did you expect from a—"

Branson's reply was interrupted by their superior, Jessica Overstreet, who entered the room with a practiced frown. "Did I miss the drop? I had to take the president's call. Was the mission a success?" She was tall, thin, and handsome in a horsey manner. She pretended taking the president's telephone call was a chore, but Bledsoe knew otherwise. Bledsoe imagined Jessica putting her stiletto another rung up the ladder of success. Up went a finger to his mouth.

"It's intense, huh? John, I see your fingernails. You're both hungry for action." Jessica chided them.

Branson brushed the powdered sugar from his shirt and Bledsoe affected a serious expression toward the boss he often called "Equal Opportunity Overstreet" behind her back. "Yes. You just missed it. All subjects down, without incident or accident. The SEALs reported the drop is complete and they're headed back to base."

"Let me boot it up so you can watch it. It's quite celebratory at the moment." Branson dusted the sugary powder from his hands and then fiddled with a computer until the scene replayed on the many large screens before them.

CHAPTER 2: The Island

Island X was as beautiful and pristine as a tiny, remote tropical spot could be. Technically an atoll that took upward of thirty million years to form, Island X was born from a volcanic explosion. Its horseshoe-shaped land surrounded coral reefs filled with flashy tropical fish in her tranquil lagoon. Being far south of the Hawaiian Islands, the balmy weather was nearly 86 degrees year-round, and placid barring any unforeseen hurricane or typhoon-caliber storms striking its low-lying elevation. The atoll's five miles were mostly inhabited by thousands of nesting and migratory seabirds (bright red frigate birds, white sooty terns, and rare boobies of all colors), coconut crabs, and wild rats, originating from who knows where. No humans. It sat untamed, untrammeled, unspoiled, and virginal in the Pacific Ocean, more than 1,000 miles from anywhere.

It's no wonder the hue and cry that abounded over the "atrocious liberal idea" of sending convicted death row inmates to such an idyllic destination, which was conveniently an unorganized territory of the United States. Of course, the location and operation were Top Secret, which meant everyone seemed to know all the details, save the island's exact coordinates. When word of the operation was leaked by a whistleblower, large segments of the American public, and people around the planet, were incensed at the mere thought of it. "The US is off her rocker sending cold-blooded killers on a one-way ticket to paradise," the typical affronted social media post read. "Maybe I should murder someone so I can go to an island. We're giving away get out of death row free cards now? This is lunacy!" someone tweeted, and it was retweeted 6,176 times. The victims' families, not receiving their promised pound of flesh, were the most poignant protesters.

But *something* had to be done, as those who had their crooked fingers positioned upward in the political winds predicted, sure as rain was coming, the US Supreme Court was going to rule yet again that the death penalty as currently executed was "cruel and unusual punishment." There were too many botched jobs at the state level alone. Too many heads catching on fire in Old Sparky. Too many prisoners in visible agony taking over an hour to die. Too many procedural delays. Perhaps, more importantly, too much money spent. That's when a novel idea, which was actually an old concept, struck—exile. Exile as a method of extreme hardship. Even though the convicts would be forever jettisoned from society, many people thought exile was too merciful, no matter the primitive conditions of no electricity, no radio or television, and no guarantee of safety.

Island X was to be the test case, with candidates selected from Terre Haute. Though the sentencing state's law governed the method of death for state crimes, for federal executions the condemned usually opted for lethal injection. Now, for a small select group, Island X was one last option. At the very last minute, when the plunger was ready to be pressed with a lethal three-drug cocktail, a handful of federal death row inmates were offered to opt instead for the enigmatic Island X. Of those offered, all but one accepted. When authorities were questioned regarding the cancelled executions, vague and dubious reasons were given: straps had worked loose, drugs were out of stock or the pharmaceutical companies weren't willing to provide the drug for lethal injection, the prisoner was dehydrated, and so on. The chosen inmates were flown to a black site in California for holding. That's when the story broke. One victim's family issued a statement: *We came to see the monster who killed our daughter put to death. To discover that he has been granted a form of clemency is beyond the pale. Our family has been victimized yet again.*

Upon accepting the offer, each reprieved prisoner sat with his attorney(s) before bulging folders filled with papers and a blue pen to sign, sign, sign—releasing claims, waiving away rights to life and limb, all for a chance to be free again. Well, free within the bounds of the island's five miles. Once deposited on the island, they were to be considered dead for all legal intents and purposes. The government owed them nothing there. Not food. Not shelter. Not medicine. Nada. They'd be forced to live off the land and govern themselves accordingly. There would be no outgoing contact with outside sources. If necessary, any contact initiated by the US government, like in a case of contagious outbreak, would be optional and at its behest.

The government populated the island's airspace with unmanned heat-seeking drones flying overhead like black birds, ensuring no prisoner moved more than one hundred feet off its outer limits, nor any other government or entity attempted entry. Sturdy metal poles sunk fifty yards off the reef held fluorescent signs declaring: _WARNING. ISLAND X. It is unlawful to enter this area without permission of the US Government. USE OF DEADLY FORCE AUTHORIZED._ At the first confirmation of trespass the weaponized drones were set to blow an individual or craft into oblivion, no questions asked and no apologies offered. There were no "boots on the ground," and other than extensive remote monitoring by the likes of agents Bledsoe, Branson, O'Neill, and their superiors, no further outlay of expense.

The US Coast Guard was informed of the island's change in operational status. As an unorganized territory, there was no Act of Congress specifying how the island could be governed. It was figuratively a black hole, chosen primarily for its seclusion. The United States ensured the location was removed from Google Earth and orbiting satellites. The chance a sailing vessel would pass by was slim, as it was naturally far removed from major shipping routes coming and going from America to Asia.

CHAPTER 3: The Drop

The SEALs had been brusque but civil. About ten minutes before Montgomery "Monty" Davenport was prepped to jump, they removed the thin cloth sack from his head, which had been loosely duct taped around his neck, so that he could get his bearings. He and his fellow red-suited prisoners were already packed and helmeted, but not with SEAL-issued parachutes as those required skill to operate. They looked like unwieldy red turtles with excess crap on their backs. Monty saw the other inmates also had their clunky box-chain handcuffs removed. Had the helicopter malfunctioned, fallen out of the sky, and they drowned in the ocean, hooded and bound by restraints, there would be no recourse, legal or otherwise, as the prisoners had already signed away life and limb.

They'd been instructed beforehand, ad nauseam, about the procedure. One Black Hawk would be following their aircraft to guarantee its safety. There would be no talking amongst themselves. Any deviation from the instructions would result in the return of the individual to the mainland (at best) or immediate death (at worst). The SEALs were positioned with their black Colt CM901s pointing at them at all times. "If you make any sudden moves we'll shoot you. Stand up when we call your name and be ready to jump. The rest of you, remain in place with your hands on your knees. If you so much as wiggle we'll kill you."

Sitting stiffly on the rumbling floor of the helicopter with his legs straight out in front of him while trying not to move this head, Monty side-glanced and got a quick look at his soon-to-be island mates. He shouldn't have been surprised to recognize a few of them from the Special Confinement Unit at Terre Haute. The SCU housed approximately fifty men, most of whom he did not know by sight, as there was not much human contact among the inmates. They were convicts, deemed not only unsuitable for civilized society, but moreover, slated for the ultimate consequence of death. His hate mail during his trials and appeals had been filled with the public's furious wrath. Anonymous letters screaming out *Oxygen thief!* scrawled in block script with blood-red felt pen served to remind him of what people thought of his continued existence. He could only imagine what the other convicts' mail was like.

The craft began to circle. As the two-windowed exit hatch opened to Monty's right, the skittish-looking inmate closest to it huddled back and clung to the inside of the helicopter with his unbound fingers. The man was slated as the first in line to jump. Two SEALs stood up the inmate, meticulously inspected and ensured the harness was secure around his crotch, under his legs and arms. They attached his parachute to the overhead static line, which would deploy the 'chute automatically upon leaving the chopper.

The remaining SEALs kept their guns trained on the others.

Second in line, a big blonde brute was sweating profusely and kept wiping his flushed face and neck on his shoulders so as not to move his hands. A thick ropy vein in his throat pulsed in time with his heartbeat. His distinctive, square-headed visage with a narrow forehead and aquiline nose looked decidedly familiar to Monty. *Ah, Hans the Cannibal. Wonderful. Fantastic. The Jew Eater. What a great time to be half Jewish!* Monty's stomach turned and threatened to bring up his oatmeal breakfast. The cannibal had entered the SCU in 2004 and was rarely spotted, as staff feared another inmate would kill him for publicity or retribution. While Monty knew the first thing he had to do was seek shelter for the first night, creating some kind of defensive weapon moved to the number one slot on Monty's subsequent island to-do list. The cannibal, using his peripheral vision, neglected to meet Monty's gaze, which unexpectedly skeeved Monty, viscerally pricking up his neck hair. Because Monty had spent twenty years on death row and seen all make and manner of humans and subhumans, the worst of the worst, he rarely got creeped out or chicken-skinned. Just as well, Monty thought, there's no use in engaging in a stare down with the cannibal and getting unnerved before the jump.

Crouched third in line and right at Monty's elbow was the youngest of the lot. Trent Doyle had been housed on the lower tier and Monty on the upper tier at SCU. Doyle was a man in his early thirties who looked as if life had chewed him up, masticated him extra long, and spit him out on a hot sidewalk. Monty detected a meth addiction from the scars of lumps, pocks, and pits sprinkling the man's face. When Doyle smiled, Monty saw he had an even set of teeth. False teeth. He probably lost them all. Chompers go all loosey-goosey on methamphetamine, and the US prison system is not known for its dental services. Doyle also had some sort of old burn on his chest creeping out the top of his shirt. But the most noticeable feature was the man's crystal-clear green eyes crinkled with crow's feet at the corners. *Friendly eyes. Thank God.* Monty nodded his chin in greeting.

To his left and fifth in line, another man Monty did not recognize intensely waited his turn. He was perhaps Monty's age and looked like he spent his time engaged in a strenuous workout program. *They probably used two sets of handcuffs on him when he was arrested.* He appeared bald as a cue ball under his helmet and his nose looked to have been broken several times. He sported little exposed skin uninked or unmolested. His hands, wrists, forearms, neck and face, even odd places, rather painful-looking places, like his eyelids, were heavily drawn in black and blue. Realistic open pupils were printed on his lids and black teardrops cascaded down onto his cheekbone. Monty pegged him as a gang member and, judging from some of the tattoos' extensive calligraphy and Aztec symbology, also Hispanic. He nodded rhythmically, as if hearing music in his head, and gazed at his tattooed fingers splayed on his thighs. Then he broke the rules by crossing himself. He'd been praying, which struck Monty as another good sign. Monty wondered if some inmates from the CMU were also included in this group.

"Don't move, Guerrero. Only warning," a SEAL barked, tensing on his gun's trigger.

Monty recognized the sixth and last man, unfortunately, a kidnapper named Shane Lubbuck. His long phallic ponytail, peeping out from his helmet, displayed little gray. Lubbuck was the last arrival to the SCU and renowned for his rotten attitude. He'd sent the prison into an uncomfortable lockdown the previous year when he attempted an escape via a drainage pipe in the recreation yard, in which he became wedged like Augustus Gloop in *Charlie and the Chocolate Factory*. Monty also knew about Lubbuck because Monty's family was slightly acquainted with his victim's family. The two degrees of criminal separation had sparked a rare letter from Monty's cousin asking about their proximity on death row.

Monty's buoyant fantasy of being on an island with white-collar criminals faded into oblivion. All in all they looked like a menagerie of rough, middle-aged convicts. *If all goes as planned, the faces of this motley crew will be the last ones I see in this life.*

Seemingly picking up on Monty's thought, a SEAL said, "Meet your new friends and your last friends." Monty imagined the SEAL probably wanted to make a joke about their lack of any impending female companionship.

"Nah, mayn, you got an island full of chicas down there for us," the tattooed fellow Guerrero wisecracked.

"There will be no chicas," the SEAL replied. "Okay, quiet. Let's roll."

The prison's custom of referring to the inmates by their names and not their prisoner numbers continued with the SEALs. Roderick Cooper's name was called. The thin, squirrelly fellow went first, meaning the SEALs had to sort of wrangle and toss him out at the last second as his fingers scrabbled at the exit door, trying to stay inside. "This is a trick," he yelped.

"Cool it, Hot Rod," a SEAL yelled while wrestling Rod's spindly foot from the wall. Rod's shoe flew out the hatch before him.

Roderick reminded Monty of his old cat, Purry Mason, desperate to escape a flea bath, bug-eyed and stretching his limbs out as far as they would go over the suds-filled sink.

Another SEAL said, "Hey, for someone who built missiles and rockets, Hot Rod sure is scared to fly!"

"I only watched tests from a bunker," he screeched back.

Roderick's knees finally gave out. His high-pitched screams on the short way down seemed to set the other convicts on edge, like when you're standing in line for a rollercoaster and someone on the ride loses their shit. A SEAL was quick to announce they'd have no more shenanigans. "One more scene like that and we'll fly back to mainland with your bodies. Hans Fritzl, step right up."

The cannibal was quick to jump of his own accord with no notable fuss except a wet, guttural grunt into the wind.

"Trent Doyle."

For style points, Trent farted loudly before he dismounted in a swan dive. Two SEALs craned out, looking down waiting to see if he hit land. "That fool almost ended up in the drink. Do not fuck around because we are not here to save you. Montgomery Davenport."

Monty thanked the SEALs before he leaped. Putting out his hand for a handshake, one just looked at him and smirked. Monty's 'chute deployed as he descended below white clouds. The visual impact of the island stole his breath. The panorama was the most beautiful sight he'd ever seen, barring the birth of his only child. Time slowed to a crawl. The atoll, rushing up to his feet, was surrounded by the most stunning shades of blue—translucent turquoise with the outer ocean a light to dark sapphire. The landmass, shaped like a horseshoe, surrounded a large lagoon. The sun, which was about an hour from setting, glinted and gleamed off the smoothing water.

On the ground, Trent was helping Rod extricate himself from his parachute. "Ho there. Hold up. You're tangled in the fabric, man," Trent yelled over the noise of the swaying palm fronds and upset birds. The fall from the sky backward had shaken

Rod, and terror left him thrashing. "Don't kick me, dude. Chill and I'll help you," Trent commanded.

Slumping in exhaustion, Rod emitted a low, forlorn whine. "Weeeeeee."

"You hurt, man?" Trent kneeled over him. "You land wrong or something?"

"It's a trap. I knew it was a trap," Rod shrieked out with a hysterical kick. "We're doomed. We're doomed. D-doomed."

"No. You're just wrapped in the 'chute." Talking fast, Trent unwound the fabric, rolled him a few times, unsnapped the buckles at Rod's chest, and loosed him from his silken cocoon. "There you go. Free as the air."

"Thank you. Oh, thank you." Rod kissed the sand in gratitude. Failing to wipe his mouth, he said, "I was scared because I can't swim. Where are we?"

Trent shook his head, looking around in amazement. "Looks like paradise."

"I can't *see* paradise. They promised to pack my glasses." Rod's cow-brown eyes blinked upward helplessly at Trent. "And my shoe is gone."

Unharnessing himself, Monty curtly nodded to Trent and Rod but didn't wait around to have a chat with the new residents. He wanted to find a sufficient hiding spot for the coming night, make a weapon, eat, and stow his goods. He doubted the newcomers would be holding an immediate summit meeting.

The US government promised it would provide each man with a survivalist training manual and rudimentary supplies—seven MREs (meals ready to eat, entrees only)—to last about a week. Because the government wasn't "animals like you." One meal a day. Seven days at best. One week to find a fresh water source or make catch basins, locate food, and set up shelter. They were told ahead of time what would be offered to them. Each prisoner only toted what could be fitted into a heavy, pre-packed backpack containing the MREs, water, a blue tarp, a change of clothes, a bandana, a twin blanket, and a Bible (optional). The only personal items they were allowed to submit were heavily vetted—family photographs, and only a dozen at that, which was another kindness. There would be no matches. The feds probably didn't want one of them setting the island ablaze without having to bust a sweat for it. If Monty knew anything from Boy Scouts, watching television, and his voracious reading while on death row, it was the importance of maintaining a fire. Fire cooked the food. Fire kept one warm. Fire disinfected things. Fire provided light in the dark and warded off insects and creatures. They'd die without it. The manual detailing the various methods to start one should be in his knapsack, if the government kept their word. The parachute's balloon or his tarp would serve him well as a rain barrier. Strategizing kept Monty from panic.

Monty had waited eight weeks for this moment.

His mind cast back to that stunning minute when he was scheduled to die. The death chamber cast an eerie light upon the tiled green walls that didn't match its white and gray mosaic floor. *Who cares about décor in a death chamber?* he thought. *Who would want that interior designer job?* The glass window for the press and his family was less than two feet away. The victims' families would be behind another (blacked-out) window. Monty stared at the ceiling. A marshal and the warden were in the room. The marshal picked up the wall phone and said to the Department of Justice Command Center, "This is the US marshal. May we proceed with the execution?" After a moment, he frowned and hung up the receiver. Monty was unstrapped from the cross-shaped brown gurney, lead into another room, and chained in front of a table. He sat stunned and shaking at the offer, which arrived within the hour.

"What's the catch?"

"No catch," the redheaded agent said smoothly.

"You want to do some weird unapproved medical testing on me? Some MK-Ultra stuff?" Monty asked him.

"No."

"Did my family have something to do with this?"

"Ha. No."

Monty was shaking so badly his signatures were illegible, which did not matter. An X would have sufficed.

After accepting his offer and being inoculated with various shots for malaria, typhoid, and tetanus, he was transferred in the following days from the SCU to a California prison. He was to be held for an indeterminate time for the other prisoners to receive their offers and be transferred for holding together to their final secret destination. During his weeks of waiting he was isolated from other inmates but allowed to read, so he mused for every hour about what he had to do to survive on an island. He also indulged himself by fattening up on canteen snacks, gaining ten pounds in the process.

Their life expectancy on the atoll, notwithstanding inevitable violence by the other residents, looked piss-poor at best. With no access to doctors or medicine they were truly in the hands of God. But, what did they have to lose?

To his chagrin, an agent named John Bledsoe informed Monty their group was a test run, and by no means the only group that could arrive. In other words, the government held the option to add another fifty convicts, or none at all, if they so desired. They could monitor deaths ("vacancies") on the island and drop more inmates at their whimsy. "Don't get comfortable," were the exact words Agent Bledsoe used.

An optimist by nature, even throughout the screwing life had given him, Monty tried to remain positive and reassured himself that any day on this side of terra firma and outside the penitentiary of Terre Haute is a blessing. His day of reckoning had been postponed.

CHAPTER 4: Humans/Unplugged

Leaving Rod, Trent, and those still landing behind, Monty jogged along the beach in his sneakers. Intermittently glancing back over his shoulder, he saw no one was following. Greedily, he sucked in his first gulps of fresh air in twenty years. Scanning for shells as he ran, he realized leaving telltale footprints wouldn't be wise if he intended to hide. The island's lush jungle was less than twenty feet to his left, beckoning him darkly. In some spots the coastline was so eroded the leafy branches, loaded down with coconuts, almost touched him. He snatched up a large, abandoned clamshell, marveling at its size, and tucked it into his pants. He dove into the thick brush filled with Pisonia trees, climbing vines, coconut palms, ferns, palmettos, and more palms. In his hurry and haste, the branches and fronds scratched and sliced into the skin of his hands and forearms as he pushed and shoved his way into the dense jungle. *Good Lord, Mont. Don't get an infected scratch right off the jump*, he thought, slowing his pace. He knocked the cobwebs off his shoulders. He was hyperventilated and high as a kite. It wasn't just the heavy tropical air that filled his nose like pure oxygen from a tank, it was the exhilaration of unbridled freedom unfelt for two decades—freedom to run, or to stop running. The sound of his racing heart pounding in his ears reminded him of his family's thoroughbred racehorses tearing up the track for a win. *Go five minutes deep*, he thought, trying to focus his spinning thoughts. *But how do you measure five minutes with no watch?* Tossing his head back he laughed, startling small creatures in the undergrowth—lizards, crickets and the like.

A thin, slick sweat covered his fifty-year-old body in a shiny sheen. The temperature was 86 degrees, as promised. Hailing originally from Palm Beach, Florida, the Sunshine State, Monty had once been accustomed to real heat, humid heat just like this. The kind that makes your thighs stick to the leather of your car's upholstery in summertime. Back in the good old days he used to sport a year-round tan too. But prison life at Terre Haute proved even hotter. With two decades in relative isolation, he'd adjusted to its environment and claustrophobia. Monty had been transferred from another federal prison and housed at the SCU when it was first constructed in 1999 under an operation code named Golden Eagle, in which the federal government consolidated their death row prisoners.

Finding a thicket he halted, taking advantage of the natural cover. Monty removed his helmet and slipped off his backpack. Hunching with his rear on his heels, so as not to soil the seat of his red pants, he unzipped the bag with trembling hands. It was filled to capacity. Smaller items were on top—his reading glasses, toiletries in a large Ziploc bag (no razor and no deodorant), a toothbrush, various chlorine and salt tablets, a tiny bottle of twenty-four count Advil, a box of individually-wrapped alcohol wipes, mosquito repellent, a bar of soap, and a hotel needle pack with colored threads, for when he needed to sew a button back on his three-piece tailored suit. He hadn't held a sewing needle in twenty years. He turned over each item, examining it as if it was precious treasure. He stared at the needle pack with its bright white, blue, black, gray, and pink string for minutes. *I'm stoned,* he thought, catching himself. *Oddly high as I've ever been. Adrenaline at its finest.* Underneath a blue 10-foot x 12-foot polypropylene tarp, which was shrink-wrapped into a small, tight square, rested the MREs, a filled water bladder, and a thin gray towel. Finally, at the bottom was the Bible—New Living Translation. Even though he was no longer religious, Monty asked for something with the Apocrypha, the hidden books of the Bible, because it lengthened the tome considerably. And who knows what use he could get out of the extra paper. Monty fished out more surprises: a pack of Bicycle standard playing cards and a mosquito net. The government was good as their word, and then some. The unexpected kindness brought tears to Monty's eyes. Unwitnessed and unwatched by any man, nestled deep in a pocket of the jungle's terrain, he wept.

Pulling himself together, he wiped his runny nose along his arm. Monty considered how to best manage his situation. He could either fashion a proper running hole for himself and his only possessions or keep everything with him at all times. Opting for the former, he located a temporary spot in the palmetto tangle and crawled in on his stomach. He twisted off the low, rotten limbs to accommodate his body, cleared an area, and lined the ground with the tarp. He unfolded the tarp into a quarter of its size and wrapped the towel over the bright blue because it blended in better with the jungle green. Since he could barely see out he figured he was hidden enough to survive the night. "Don't fling me in dat briar patch," he joked aloud, like Br'er Rabbit. He shrugged out of his sticky red top and pants, leaving on only his white undershirt and boxer shorts.

At first Monty tried to ignore the paper-cut stings on his arms, but then he decided to open up an alcohol wipe and clean the scratches. It stung like hell. He used every bit of one swab until it was bone-dry and placed it back in its pack and stowed away the trash. While there was still daylight he decided to eat an MRE. He shifted through the options: chicken pesto pasta, fried rice, macaroni and beef sauce, Asian beef strips, beef ravioli, and pork sausage with gravy. As this could be his last meal, he picked what he liked the most out of the selection—macaroni and beef sauce. Though the MREs had a shelf life of up to three years, Monty doubted he'd live that long.

The macaroni and beef entrée required heating. Never having prepared an MRE, this was his first adventure on the island. He opened the box and tore open the green wrapper that housed the heating element at the bottom. Using the water from his water bladder, he gingerly poured a small amount up to the marked line to start the heating process. He slid in the pouch and used a nearby lava rock to angle the nested packages at a 45-degree angle. While it cooked, he scouted outside his briar patch for rocks to fashion a weapon. Inmates are quite crafty in their abilities to transform one thing into another. He'd seen batteries made into cuff keys, shanks from toothbrushes, compressed and molded paper squeezed into "water sticks" that could beat someone senseless, and ballpoint pens made into tattooing machines. He thought a sharp shell would make an excellent starter weapon with little effort. Squatting over, he struck the clamshell with a rock, hoping to create a cutting edge. But the shell shattered into many odd curvy pieces, none of which seemed effective for a weapon.

He saw a black object whip by at the tree line. Squinting, he focused on the small, bird-shaped drone. They'd likely been flying around the whole time, but with all the other sights to behold he'd failed to notice. It was noiseless and, but for its movement, unobtrusive. Monty waved at it.

The steaming package got his attention. Picking up the bag, he managed to burn the tips of his fingers in the process. He gritted his teeth to keep from yelping. He opened the plastic spork, mixed the concoction, and feasted. It had a high note of chili powder. While it wasn't fine dining at Chez Jean-Pierre, it wasn't half bad. Better than prison food.

The sounds of the jungle were as pervasive as its heat. To Monty's ears, the crashing waves were straight ahead. The singing of insects came at him in three dimensions. The jungle's dominant smell was oceanic and earthy: that of fish, beach, wet rotting compost, and seductive floral scents. He was overwhelmed by stimuli. The first brilliant sunset he experienced was odd, quick. Viewed through the trees, it was as if the great orb of an orange eye winked once like a sultry vixen then dropped under the Earth, leaving him in utter pitch-darkness. The night was cloudy, a blackness he never before experienced. As he couldn't see the stars, or a hand in front of his face, he felt he'd be relatively safe until daylight.

In the dark, he pondered. In his strategy to stay alive, Monty knew he had to show no weakness or fear or the others might play upon it. Feeling vulnerable, Monty weighed the five men he was up against—a cannibal, rapists, murderers, terrorists, and who knows what else if what they were convicted of was a small sample of their crimes. Men who may behave lawlessly, like untamed animals, when given their liberty. These men are hardcore, none of them doddering old fogies. If he was physically attacked, Monty surmised he could take the jittery one called Cooper and maybe the friendly-eyed meth imbiber Doyle. Even if they both were younger, they looked soft. The kidnapper, Lubbuck, was a question mark. The gang member and Hans the cannibal gave him harder pause. The cannibal, easily a decade younger than Monty, was a big man and looked as if he wouldn't blink if hit over the head with a log. Guerrero was beyond fit, and with all his tattoos he obviously had a high pain tolerance.

Monty also assumed the others would be lowbrow and coarse in speech, morals, and habits. He knew from the prison guards that a few of the SCU prisoners were downright difficult—namely Lubbuck—and were kept away from the others. He knew the adjoining CMU prisoners were held for terrorism-related crimes. If he were smart, he'd fly under the radar by dropping any remnants of his cultivated manners and try to keep his head down. Living in prison he had learned the lingo and its ways, but had not totally scrubbed off the last of his breeding and refinement because he never wanted to do so. It was like an old patina on his soul and the only thing left of his true self. *Good luck with that,* he thought, tamping down pangs of pride.

Hopefully, one of them would set a practical tone so he wouldn't have to broach the subject. He prayed there was a chance for democratic order and that their basest instincts for food, water, and shelter wouldn't arouse the primitive, turning them into savages in a fight for survival. He curled up and used his pack as a pillow. With his habitual insomnia, the island's continual rustling of leaves, a wind that moaned complainingly, and the night creatures singing their songs, Monty did not sleep well. His apprehension magnified every sound. There was no silence for the hunted.

When he finally dozed off, he fell into a dream. It was execution day and he was strapped onto the gurney again. Everything was exactly the same. According to the wall clock, it was 7:04 a.m. He was on his back looking up, riveted by a water stain, the shape of which looked like a vampire bat—a wonky one from an old Bela Lugosi film. Monty's thought was that his last musings were about the shape of a trivial, moldy brown stain on a prison ceiling. The wrist and leg straps were almost too tight and cutting off his circulation. The guards opened the heavy curtains to reveal a viewing window. Sweat slid down his temples. He swallowed hard. He was trying to say his last words but no sound came out. Then the phone didn't ring. The marshal didn't frown. The needle slid into the tubing, the solution running into his arm. Everything slowed. The molecules lifted from his feet first, hovering. His spirit floated above his body and gazed down in curiosity.

That's when he realized he was dead and the island was a fantasy, a hallucination created by an oxygen-deprived mind.

CHAPTER 5: Fire

Monty awoke to chitter of morning birdsong. It took a minute for him to get his bearings. *I am really here on an island.* Since he was damp all over, he changed back into the red pants and packed away both his white T-shirt and shorts. He thanked God for being alive when he found the photographs he'd requested of his daughter, Chelsea, tucked throughout his Bible. He thumbed the edges of an old snapshot of him holding her, her blonde head cuddled in the crook of his arm. She was snuggling her favorite stuffed animal, a beloved well-handled yellow and black bumblebee. Through the years, Chelsea had become more and more removed from him both physically and emotionally. But this picture did not reflect that. *Prison is for criminals, not little children*, he reminded himself. He tried never to add more to her emotional burden at having a dead mother, and a father sentenced for it. Chelsea's last letter to him was on Crane stationary and said simply, *I am getting married to Douglas. Wish you could be here.*

To the best of his ability, Monty repacked his backpack, leaving out the thin gray towel. It was time to make a move. He followed the crash of the surf. Seeing how everything looked similar, and how easy it would be to lose track of his belongings in the jungle, he decided to stow the goods wrapped in the blanket at the shoreline behind a crooked tree. He placed a conch shell beside its base to serve as a marker.

Monty walked barefoot along the magnificent coastline back toward the landing spot with his mind still reeling. The tang of salt was on his lips. A light breeze lifted his thinning hair and caressed his handsome face. He strode briskly with long, wide treads enjoying the sensation of his toes sinking into the sand. He felt keenly alive to the sights and smells around him. A drone whizzed by from behind, continuing in his direction.

Almost blinded by the light dazzling on the waves and a sudden swarm of gnats, he could barely detect Trent, Guerrero, and Lubbuck, naked and off in the distance. *Late making friends and influencing people?* Monty mused. He walked with his back as straight as a ramrod. As he got closer he offered a wave of his hand, as civilized people do, to the three men looking at him. He considered the SEALs likely chose this area for the landing because it seemed to have an extended coastline. In other places the dense brush and coconut palms stretched almost horizontally across the sand reaching toward the sun and water.

Given the drying towels hanging on the palms, it appeared the men had taken a dip in the ocean. They were now attempting to start a fire in a viable spot on the beach, which was smart because starting one in the jungle would be pure folly if it sparked out of control.

"Sleep well, pilgrims?" Monty offered them in a chipper greeting. His white plastic spork, the handle sharpened to a fierce point on the rock well into the night, was wound into the back of his red pants, which he also rolled up to the knees.

"Like a free man who cheated death." Guerrero spoke in wonderment, slapping his nude, wet chest, which featured an inked rosary chain. "Never thought I'd see the day. Thanks to the Man upstairs and the Holy Mother." Guerrero crossed himself, kissed his fingers, and motioned skyward, which Monty recognized as a sort of Catholic gesture. Guerrero sported a customized du-rag which he crafted himself. "Why you run off?" he asked.

"I wanted to experience freedom," Monty replied.

The man named Trent chimed in. "Yeah. I get you. We can move freely now. We don't have to wait at cages or doors no more because there are no doors. I hate doors. We can eat and sleep when we want. No more routines. No more fire alarms. No more strobe lights. There are bugs here but they tossed in some bug spray." Trent scratched his skin. "I still got ate up to hell and back."

"Tshh. Tell me about it. Zancudo—los mosquitoes as big as chupacabras." Guerrero measured an immense circular area with his hands over his head like a busted ballerina in fifth position. His smile was as large. Monty grinned back.

"What's a chupacabra?" Trent asked him.

"A bloodsucking monster!" Guerrero opened his eyes wide and bared his teeth in a caricature of a vampire.

They all laughed freely, real and relieved laughs. Monty could scarcely believe his luck. *How entertaining; we have convicts with a sense of humor here*. He thought of how in many ways prisoners deaden their feelings to survive. Perhaps the shared, giddy outpouring of emancipation, coupled with the invigoration of the open ocean air, explained their good-natured attitudes. Whatever the reason, it was a damn good sign.

"I'm Monty from the SCU," he told the trio. Inmates always went by their last names in the Terre Haute prison and Monty wanted no more of it. "I never want to hear my surname, my last name, again. So, please call me Monty."

"I recognize your face. I'm Trent Doyle," the tweaker replied.

"My dear guests, I'm Mr. Lazarus, your host. Welcome to Fantasy Island," Guerrero stated. Missing the 1970s television reference, the others looked quizzical. "I'm not going by any old names. I'm reborn like Lazarus. From now on I'll be Lazarus. Lazarus!" Guerrero yelled to the clouds. There was no echo. The wind simply stole the name and carried it swiftly away.

"Where are you from? Terre Haute?" Monty asked the newly minted Lazarus.

"Yeah. They had me at the CMU to control me. Me and a bunch of Al-Qaeda."

Monty turned to the kidnapper. "You're Lubbuck, right?"

Lubbuck lifted his chin. "Buck. Short for Lubbuck."

The obvious diminutive, Monty thought, forgetting he also chose the shortened version of his own name. "Where are the other two?" Monty raised an eyebrow at the jungle.

"The cannibal took to the woods like his ass was on fire. Hot Rod...who knows," Trent replied.

"Como alma que lleva el diablo (which was Spanish for 'running as if his soul was possessed by the devil'). He crazy, that one," Lazarus declared. "He come from the CMU too."

"I think the drones freaked him out, electronics and all that," Trent said. "Remember he was the one on the other unit we'd hear scream clear across the buildings when the lights flickered or the power surged. He's that guy. After I helped him out of his 'chute he was jabbering like mad about drones. I looked up, there they were, and poof he was gone." Trent was still digging vigorously at his arms with his fingernails.

"I had a drone trained on me last night," Monty said. "It sat on a branch like a bird."

"They're all over the place. Infested," Lazarus said. "Yo, we're thrust on this island with a fucking cannibal, mayn. A fucking chomo cannibal." Chomo was shorthand slang for child molesters. "He was with you guys in your unit. You know about him, right?" Lazarus moved from foot to foot almost in a dance. "When we run outta food he's already got us scouted, foraged and picked out spices. Fuck that." He opened his eyes extra wide so the whites showed all around. "I'm not gonna be that freak's last meal, you know what I mean? Why they put him with us? He needs to enjoy the air he breathin' 'cause I'm marking him."

"You can say that again," Buck agreed, spitting on the ground.

"I believe in the resurrection of the dead, and I'm not crawling out of his asshole when the bugle blows, you know?" Lazarus said.

"A trumpet blows," Trent corrected him. "At the end of the world it's a trumpet. Seven trumpets."

"Trumpet, bugle...pffft. What's the difference?" Putting his curled fingers to his lips, Lazarus bugled out some whimsical notes. The words "Vida loca" were spelled out on the tops of his fingers, on all but his thumbs. It was obvious Lazarus had already befriended Trent and took no offense at being corrected.

At least I won't be bored with this lot, Monty thought.

As Lazarus and Trent resumed assessing the dryness and rottenness of various pieces of wood, Buck tried to bust open a fallen coconut with a stick.

"Put it on a tarp so that if you crack it you'll capture the juice," Monty offered.

Buck looked at Monty but said nothing. He calmly took his stick and whacked the coconut with great force, cracking it open. "*If* I crack it..." He lifted the fruit to his mouth, sucked out the remaining juice, and declared it, "Better than the milk from your sister's titty."

"I don't have a sister," Monty replied, unfazed.

Buck tossed the empty coconut and bragged, "I tagged a drone last night with one of these."

That's so wasteful, Monty thought, chewing the inside of his cheek. Turning to Lazarus and Trent, Monty said, "I was going to start a fire but I'm not as young as I used to be and, heh, hopefully this isn't like *Lord of the Flies*. Want some help?" Monty really wanted to say, "We have to help each other. If we don't, we'll die," but he knew acting like a leader could quickly sight a bull's-eye on his back, or his front, with this group.

"I can start fire," Lazarus stated. "Don't believe me? Watch." Lazarus seized a dry branch and snapped it in half over his knee manfully. He pressed Trent into service. "Yo, find more old branches like this one. The others are too soft. And look for a sharp rock the size of my fist."

Monty clicked his fingers and said, "Hey wait, I have eyeglasses." He ran back to his stashed supplies to fetch his spectacles and ripped a few blank pages from the back of his Bible. He was elated to have the tool to start fire and be the hero of the day. But his effort was in vain. Contrary to common belief, using his glasses to start a fire didn't work. Not on this island. No matter the angle, the suddenly weak rays passing through the glasses to the paper were ineffectual and not an auspicious beginning.

Buck laughed at Monty's futile efforts. Lazarus said, "Maybe the Bible won't catch fire. Maybe God don't want you desecrating no Bible."

Using a rock, Lazarus started rubbing a foot-long flat plane into a long branch. When he finished he honed a thinner groove atop it. His muscles and sinews bulged with the effort. This was the hardest method for fire starting. "I've been readin' those survival books like a monk."

Monty thought, of anyone, Lazarus couldn't possibly look less like a monk. Monty offered to stabilize the end of the branch, placing his knee down to keep it from rolling around as Lazarus continued to rub and scrape and rub. At Lazarus's continued urging of "More fiber, yo," Trent went searching for and gathered the driest, busted open coconut for its exposed fiber and more firewood. Trent whistled as he wandered about—that tune from *The Bridge on the River Kwai,* on repeat.

He's the whistler, Monty groaned inwardly. At the SCU, Monty used to bury his head in a pillow when he heard the familiar chipper notes sound from the tier below. Monty assumed it was a guard's idea of torture.

"Let me take over for a minute," Monty kept offering. Lazarus, sweat dripping into his eyes, stubbornly labored for another twenty minutes until he finally relented to Monty's help. After taking turns at rubbing back and forth between them, their heads inclined over the sticks, the end of the groove finally started to smoke from friction. The island was thick with humidity and the wood was soft.

Meanwhile, with Buck's aid, Trent fashioned the gathered wood and dried coconut husks into an open pyramid shape. Trent muttered to Buck, "Don't stack the wood. Stand it up to let the oxygen flow through."

Monty gently nudged the fiber closer to the end of the hot groove as Lazarus drove the rock into the wood. "Come on. Come on, coño. Come on!" The curls of smoke taunted them mercilessly. They hoped every next stroke would be the one to start a blaze. They chattered urging each other on. "We're almost there!" For another quarter hour it refused to flame, only teased them instead with faint wisps. When the cherry finally sparked, Lazarus knocked the coal into the fiber. Monty used the ripped pages from his Bible to flash the red coal into a quick blaze, and when they tossed the flame on the log pile it fed noisily on the tinder.

"Good job. Not bad for a merry band of outcasts," Monty declared in satisfaction after the flames spread by consuming the fiber and licking the piled wood.

The roaring and spitting fire, and their high-spirited, deep-throated yips, drew Hot Rod from the jungle's depths like a wonky moth. Unlike the others, who did not have their packs out in the open, Rod toted his knapsack and scanned the sky warily, still agitated.

Lazarus began teasing immediately. "Yo, Hot Rod, what did the drone say?"

"Don't call me that, Guerrero. No. No. My name is Roderick Cooper or Roddy or just Rod." He was not amused. He was twisting the top of his short black hair until it stuck up straight in the air every which way.

"Well, I'm Lazarus now. No more Guerrero. My new name symbolizes who I wanna be—risen from the dead and reborn."

Rod looked at Monty. "I know about you. You're Montgomery Davenport the III. And I know you, Shane Lubbuck. And I know about Hans Fritzl too. Wh—where is Hans Fritzl?" Behind his glasses, Rod's dark brown eyes were like two large and fragile teacups. His skin was white as a corpse with the typical death row pallor they all shared.

"What's wrong? Afraid of getting eaten?" Trent asked. The word eaten sounded like 'et.'

"Who isn't?" Rod said fretfully. He eyed them all in turn. There was a long ironic silence. No answer was the answer. The fire popped and hissed.

"I was looking for my shoe." Rod remained at a healthy distance, like a feral cat that would run at the slightest movement. "Are you sure we haven't died? What if this is what happens after you die?" Rod ventured hesitantly.

Lazarus hooted. "Does this look like Heaven?" He answered himself. "Hell, maybe it is. Maybe it's a halfway point like purgatory. But there's no fire in purgatory." Lazarus scratched his forehead in thought.

"You're alive, dude," Trent declared. "Do you see your shadow?"

"Yes," Rod replied, looking behind him to his long, thin frenetic twin. "Yes, I do. Good. I just want to make sure this isn't some mocked-up place—an illusion."

"The dead cast no shadow, so you're alive," Trent said.

The logic seemed to convince Rod, who moved closer to the fire and stretched out his hands for unnecessary warmth. The men stood around it in a circle.

Monty broke the ice. "So, what's the plan, fellas? We're all here now, except the cannibal."

"The plan is there is no plan," Buck stated bluntly, raising his left eyebrow as if the question was ludicrous. He scratched his balls with impudence.

"Um, stay alive?" Trent mumbled.

"Staying alive," Lazarus sang, rolling his fingers in his best imitation of John Travolta discoing to the Bee Gees. They would soon discover Lazarus liked to talk in song lyrics. Butchered song lyrics. "My plan is to catch pescado and kick up my heels. And appreciate each grain of sand, wave, and even los mosquitoes. You know what I mean?"

"Uh-huh." Trent laughed. "All but the mosquitoes."

Feeling the men out, Monty weighed his words. "Well, my plan is to coexist—don't put your hands on me and I won't put my hands on you."

"Good," Rod said. "I like that. Mind our own business. Yes. Yes. That sounds right to me. And it starts with the government still surveilling us." He pointed to the sky and approached closer to the others, whispering. "They use ARGUS, which is a 1.8 billion pixel video stream. All the moving images are tracked and they can see us right now on their computer screens. They don't even need these smaller drones. The smaller drones and mavs—that stands for micro-air vehicles—can be used for visual surveillance, tagging, targeting...everything. They can fly over us high up. They can just loiter around. Watching us. Listening to us. Right now they see us."

Monty's mother had a name for people like Rod—worryguts. Monty sighed. "Can we leave that life behind? They've been watching us for years, real up close and personal, up my ass. I assume they'll leave us to our own devices. So, let's not look back."

Trent agreed. "Man, what could they want from us other than us staying put? We are a handful of washed-out old misfits. If they wanted our silence, we'd be dead." He counted heads and added one for the cannibal. "Six times over."

"But why did they drop us here? I don't trust their reasoning, or l-lack thereof," Rod said. "Why us six out of fifty men at Hot Terror? I don't trust them. Look. I dug out a microchip." He lifted his sleeve, displaying a bloody gouge. "Yeah, when they gave me those injections for malaria and tetanus, they didn't think I would notice the one with the microchip. Did they give you guys injections?"

"A microchip? In a needle?" Buck laughed. "That's ridiculous."

"I dug it out with a broken Coke bottle. It was a little black speck. I put it in a shell and tossed it out to sea. Let them track that."

"Wait, they can microchip pets, can't they?" Monty said. "Maybe we are a sociological experiment."

"Well, why are there no brothers or Al-Qaeda here then?" Trent wondered. "Only whites and a

Puerto Rican. That's not much of an experiment. That's hinky."

Rod nodded as if he understood being fooled.

"It's The Man's usual racism," Buck stated. "I don't trust people either. I trust things. I like this island." Buck slouched. "She and I are gonna get along just fine. They are gonna have to pry me off of her."

"I reckon none of us know what's really going on," Monty said.

CHAPTER 6: Catching the Break

Trent demonstrated an aptitude of self-reliance when he brought a large coconut crab to the fire. With childish glee he yelled, "Look! Crab!" He yanked off an uneven claw, waving it about. "Look at this beast. It's like some prehistoric creature. It's a meal in itself."

Inspecting Trent's crab, Lazarus hooted in delight. "Dios mio! Rustle up some crab."

"Why is everything so enormous?" Monty asked.

"I reckon there's no pollution here, nothing artificial. They're living away from chemicals and manmade bullshit. And the sea hasn't been farmed into near extinction," Trent replied.

Monty scratched behind his ear. "How do you plan to cook it? Normally, it would boil in a pot, which we don't have. If the fire was down to coals, which it isn't, we could use a plastic Ziploc bag to boil it."

"Have you seen a flat rock around?" Trent toyed with the living crab, which attempted to pinch him with its remaining claw.

"I'm sure there's a few thousand somewhere," Monty said.

"We can cook on a flat rock by placing it right next to a log on the fire. The rock absorbs the heat, transfers it to the food, and then cooks the food. Presto!"

Trent didn't need to search far since the beach offered a suitable small slab of stone. As he tested out his technique, they captured more crustaceans and joined him in gorging themselves on land crab. With his face stuffed full of food, Trent reminded Monty of his daughter's hamster. Lazarus picked up a tune, a rap chestnut called "Gitmo North," which was the nickname for the CMU. Even Rod nodded along.

Basking in the glow of a good meal, Trent leaned back in satisfaction. "The only thing more perfect would be if I was faded and kickin' it right here. Even some fermented apple juice would be nice. Can alcohol be made out of coconuts?"

"You need sugar." Lazarus tanned his olive skin in the sun. "We can smoke though, if we find something to smoke."

"We're like pioneers in a new frontier." Monty picked his teeth with a fingernail.

Buck raised his chin. "What is this place? Where are we?"

"I reckon we're on a pinpoint in the ocean," Trent replied, looking up at the passing clouds.

"Well, tell me something I don't know," Buck said.

So Monty began. "In Hawaii, a long time ago, they had places designated as Puuhonua where refugees could flee to avoid death. We are not in Hawaii though. About our location, my attorney was able to tell me this: there were two shipwrecks on this island nearly a century apart. I believe both vessels were blown off course and got hung up on the coral reefs. Apparently, the reefs out there are really jagged and sharp, treacherous, and it's hard to gauge the water's depth. The way in via the channel is also difficult. You have to hit it at just the right wind and tide to get inside. I think it was his way of telling me there's no escape. Well, a long time ago a ship called the *Albatross* got hung up and the crew made it to shore, but they were found dead later on the island all scattered around here and there willy-nilly. A dozen souls all strewn around haphazardly. On the ship, the captain's log noted the presence of aggressive sharks and how the crew hoped to make it by swimming to shore but there were no other clues. They made it to land, but something happened to them once they arrived."

Lazarus frowned. "That's creepy. Like a ghost story. That's a fucked up thing for your lawyer to tell you."

Trent jumped up in excitement. "Hey! Maybe this place is haunted. Woooo."

Monty chuckled. "Maybe a haunting would do us good. Scare the devil out of us, as my grandmother used to say. But people are more dangerous than ghosts."

"No. The EMFs, they are more dangerous," Rod declared, emphatically shaking his head from side to side. He hadn't spoken for an hour.

Trent squinted at Rod. "The what?" Trent sat in the path of the smoke's fire to avoid the mosquitoes.

"EMFs. Electromagnetic fields from the old volcano below us. The volcano is a conduit. Can't you feel the greater frequencies? It affects humans, like our sleep patterns and our functioning," Rod explained with increasing manic enthusiasm. He snapped his fingers and twisted his hair while trying to explain. "You know, like the Bermuda Triangle. Back home I disconnected from all the EMFs I could. They do strange things, very strange, powerful things."

"Are you saying we're in the Bermuda Triangle?" Buck raised his eyebrow at Rod. "C'mon, you are full of shit. We are nowhere near it. We didn't fly that far."

"Not the actual Bermuda Triangle, a place like the Bermuda Triangle." Rod's tone was tinged with alarm. "A place where things go away, go missing forever."

Buck dismissed him out-of-hand. "That's just superstition. See what you started?" he said to Monty.

Monty knew he had to say something, so he angled gently. "My attorney also told me the feds may eventually drop more Row convicts. Maybe." Monty shrugged in faux nonchalant indifference. By using the old 'us against them' mentality, he thought mentioning the threat of others coming could bond the group together in an alliance.

"Yeah, like women?" Buck smiled sarcastically. "Are those the kind of tales your high-priced attorneys told you? You fell for that hook, line, and one hefty sinker!"

"Right. That ain't gonna happen," Trent agreed. "They ain't gonna put women here, even criminal ones, to get pregnant and subject innocent children to us. Remember that SEAL said there wouldn't be chicas."

"Didn't they tell any of you about other inmates coming?" Monty asked again. He tried to read the men's body language. Trent rubbed the bottom of his chin stubble back and forth; Lazarus was crouched with his fingers steepled; Buck was leaning back; and Rod was still twirling his hair. They looked doubtful.

"No," Trent said.

"Hmm," Monty mumbled. "Interesting."

"Didn't your suits give you the scoop on where exactly we're at?" Buck asked, his voice laced with contempt.

Monty felt a stinging dislike for Buck. "No," Monty replied, straining to be civil. "I told you all I know. What did your attorney say?"

Buck snorted. "My public defender? He was some random guy who came in and didn't say shit except 'sign here, here, and here.' You are probably the only one of us with his own private attorney and a number after your name—III, IV, V, whatever."

"Three," Rod added.

Monty stared at Buck, who failed to blink. Rod was digging aimlessly in the sand and accidentally flicked a handful at Lazarus, who wiped the grains away. "S-sorry."

Rod regarded Lazarus's face, tilting his head to the side. "I've never really looked at your face before," he remarked innocently. "Those black tear drops." He traced a finger down his own cheek. "Does that mean you were in a gang?"

Buck rolled his eyes at Rod. "It means he killed someone."

Lazarus snorted and puffed out his chest. "Gang? Pshh. It was a brotherhood, like a religion. We looked after each other. My cousin, QuiQue, jumped me in when I was twelve."

"Did you kill three people then?" Rod's eyes widened with the question. His right hand darted protectively over his heart.

"Just snitches," Lazarus said, almost cheerfully. "People who can't do their time but they wanna play the game. Yo, I beat one snitch like he ruined Christmas. I pinata'd his ass. I hit him so hard the earring fell out of his ear. I slit another snitch's neck after I broke one knife off in his ribs. The third earned a buck fifty. In my world, betrayal is a capital crime. That's all I will say. Except maybe they want me here." He pointed to the sky like Rod had done. "My reach on the Row was too long, that's why I was in the unit with all those terrorists." He stretched his tattooed arm out in demonstration of length. "That's all I say."

"I was at SCU for two years. Two years of hell was enough for me. What were you in for?" Buck asked Trent, not even bothering to hint around.

Trent snorted. "Two years? Cry me a river."

Lazarus started singing the Justin Timberlake song.

Trent downplayed his crime. "Drugs." He fiddled with his white T-shirt, which partially covered a heinous chest scar. He deflected and stood up. "I'm gonna get some more husks on the fire to keep the 'skeeters away."

"That ain't all. C'mon, what drugs you play with?" Buck prompted further.

"Meth, mostly. That's how it started…" Trent's voice trailed off.

Rod chimed in. "Wow. Those cold medications can be pretty toxic. Drug companies poison people."

Trent laughed edgily. "The only non-toxic ingredient is the pseudoephedrine. Okay. My bit was for a bank robbery. Some fool in line was carrying concealed and pulled on me so I shot him. It was a reflex. He died. So did a bank customer, but I didn't touch her. She was shot by the police from outside and they pinned that on me too. Said a bullet ricocheted off a wall or something. So I caught the blame for the po-po's bad aim. That was bad luck for her, and me. Worst day of my life." Trent's voice held no notes of contrition. He fingered his chest scar.

"What did you do, Mr. Librarian? Kill a fly? Why did the SEAL boys call you Hot Rod?" Buck looked condescendingly at Rod, who quickly shook his head at Buck.

"No. No. I'm not saying anything about it because they are watching and they can hear and see everything we say. Look. There's a drone right there!" Rod jumped up. "My brain is like a radio receiver."

"Good. Tune in to classic rock," Lazarus said. "Rod blew up a government building with some people in it," he informed the others.

"Oh yeah? Why d'ya do that, Hot Rod?" Buck asked.

Rod shook his head in distress.

Monty calmly tried to reason with them. "What does it matter? We're reprieved now. Take it easy." Monty said to Lazarus, "Don't start singing the Eagles."

Lazarus changed tack. "Rod's right; the past is past. Don't say anything they can use to snitch out other people. All you need to know about my history is right here." He beat his chest proudly and gestured to his inked skin. "Like these ojos, my eyes, they are always wide open."

"So, is past the past with the cannibal too?" Trent squinted into the sun.

For the first time on the island Lazarus lost his cheerful composure. He shook his head. "Oh hell no. Cannibal has no morals. Killing little girls and children is uncalled for. That is chomo shit." Lazarus pointed his finger. "One of those little girls could have been my little Lourdes. I got grandchildren."

Monty, knowing Buck's criminal history, carefully observed Buck and said nothing. On alert, Buck looked Lazarus up and down then threw a twig into the fire.

"Chomo is food now, understand?" Lazarus added.

Apparently, gang members have rules—hard and fast rules—like no raping, no child molesting, and no child killing. Lazarus had principles and he'd kill Hans, and perhaps Buck too, purely on principle.

Before anyone could turn the tables on Buck and vigorously quiz him about his misdeeds, Monty changed the subject. "Hey, I can't believe I'll never have to wear those fancy silver bracelets again."

"H'yeah. Your Rolex? Who did you bite while lying in the lap of luxury?" Not appreciating the subject change, Buck jeered at Monty. "I bet you're from one of those fancy-pants families that eat eggs from cups and have bedrooms no one ever slept in." His jokey undertone barely masked his disgust.

Monty felt a flush rising to his cheeks but he bit his tongue, which was no easy task for him. "I think you have an idealized notion about my family. In a nutshell, my wife and two federal agents were murdered in my home, while I was there. I have no recollection of any of it. I don't know what transpired. I think someone else must have done it, but the doctors surmised I did it in a fugue state—amnesia."

"I read about heroin and ice picks," a shuddering Rod added to Monty's story.

"Heroin, huh?" Buck chuckled.

"It was an occasional vice," Monty said. "I kept that ape caged."

"Umhmmm," Buck said.

"Whoa. You're that Ice Pick Killer," Lazarus said, eyes wide. "You don't look the type."

"What does that type look like?" Monty asked.

"Then your cousin ran for political office later?" Rod said.

Monty pinched the bridge of his nose at the questioning. "That he did. He lost and blamed my conviction for spoiling his political aspirations. He runs a super PAC now. What else do you want to know?"

Therein followed a freewheeling conversation that covered everything from how close each had come to the needle, what everyone's last meal had been, if they'd had one, and whether they'd been allowed to shower or make any last phone calls before being shipped off to the island.

"So who was the first of us to get an offer?" Trent wondered. "Who here was fixin' to die?"

"My time was up," Rod jabbered. "When they told me that I didn't have to die I was almost disappointed. I didn't take a last meal because I was on a hunger strike."

"Who could eat? I was almost toast too. The guards were pushing the air out of the needle when the phone rang at the last possible second." Sweating at the memory, Monty wiped his neck. "I'm pretty sure the cook ate my last meal."

"Once I got my offer I started eating like a wild animal." Buck sneered. "That's one thing I won't miss, prison slop. I had a few years left but I woulda busted out of there...again." Buck had already bragged about his first prison break attempt.

Lazarus said, "My date was for April of next year. A few years back, I had last rites and last visits, then won an appeal. I will miss mi familia."

"Is that your brotherhood?" Rod asked.

"Nah. The family—the wife, kids, grandkids. I got two boys and one girl. Nine grandchildren too."

"I have a daughter named Chelsea," Monty said. "I can't believe I'll never see her again."

"My mother is still alive and I have a sister. They don't communicate with me anymore," Rod said. "They disconnected from me, which was for the best."

"I have two kids and two baby mommas," Trent said.

Buck did not offer comment on his family, so Lazarus remarked on Buck's name tattoos. "Tiffani, Beth, and Ann Marie. Those your daughters?"

"I ain't gonna lie. They are just women." Buck winked. "It's amazing what bitches will send a prisoner if you tattoo their name on yourself, especially married ones. Commissary money and pictures in sappy love letters." When Monty rolled his eyes, Buck snapped back. "Respect my hustle. Not everyone had money, family, or a trust funding their lifestyle."

They talked into the night about prison things and comparing the different units.

"Remember that one Arab dude in CMU who went loco and cut off his own testicle?" Lazarus performed an animated reenactment of the deed.

They chatted along to the sound of rocks scraping and grinding against rocks as each fashioned his own knife, contemplating how they got there and what had stayed vengeance's hand.

CHAPTER 7: Antonio Guerrero (aka Lazarus)

Antonio Guerrero spent a ten-year stint on federal death row for the premeditated murder of two people and the attempted premeditated murder of a third. He was raised in a gang family and no stranger to the state penitentiary. Savvy and relentless, he was able to stay abreast of the gang's affairs during his numerous incarcerations. Antonio and his accomplice, a cousin, were convicted in Arizona for the killing of multiple gang members. His three victims, all related to each other, were in the Federal Witness Protection Program after they turned on his organization and testified in court. The Marshal Service had issued the witnesses new identities with new jobs and new lives, but Guerrero and his cousin rooted out and slaughtered them. Guerrero was loyal to the end. After sentencing, he was transferred to the United States Federal Penitentiary at Terre Haute and placed in the CMU with terrorists like those from Guantanamo Bay because of his ability to communicate with gang members on the outside.

CHAPTER 8: The Blue Lagoon

It wasn't necessary to climb trees to access the coconuts. The men amassed a goodly amount of the fruit by simply picking it from the low-hanging trees that grew sideways across the sand.

Being uninhabited, the island only had natural paths carved out by the wind, eroded by water, or traversed by creatures. In searching for the lagoon, which they knew to be in the middle of the island, the men cut a line into the jungle with their bare hands. Aiming for the center, they started a new path toward the water by snapping, wrenching and twisting off limbs, tearing out vines, and ripping away flora, travelling through various stands of trees. Keeping a watchful eye, Rod dawdled behind the others and went out of his way to avoid trampling a plant or a flower, a kindness, a delicateness the others were lacking. Monty used a walking stick to keep the branches from whipping him in the face, and also for knocking down the webs of enormous brown spiders. It took them twenty minutes of bushwhacking to reach the lagoon. As it emptied into the open sea via a small channel, they could have just as easily walked around the miles of coastline to locate its overgrown entrance. To their surprise, the lagoon was more beautiful than the exterior of the atoll.

Buck wiped his forehead with his soiled T-shirt. "I'm parched. Is this also salt water?"

"Yep," Trent said.

"I didn't get no seven days' worth of water in my pack," Buck complained. "More like two days."

"Some people can live weeks without food, but not water," Trent said, worried. "A human needs to drink at least eight liters per day to function and that's not factoring in sweating like pigs. Not getting enough water will kill us quicker than anything. We'll die off like flies."

"He's right. He's right. I've gone nine days without eating. They used to force a tube down my throat after a week," Rod mumbled. "But I had to drink."

"So where's the fresh water?" Buck asked.

"There isn't any, except rain," Trent said.

"Perhaps the easiest way to collect potable water would be to use one of the blue tarps or a parachute," Monty began.

At the word 'potable' Buck mouthed in silent mockery behind Monty.

"I was thinking we could string up a tarp by the holes and slope it down to the ground like a funnel using gravity to our advantage. Then we could use some vessel like an empty coconut or a helmet to catch the rain." Monty chose his words and tone carefully so his comments would not be interpreted as pushy or commanding. With his walking stick he drew a proposed diagram on the ground. "What do you guys think?"

Trent offered a different twist on the theme. "Actually, let the tarp catch the water and use a shell to scoop it out when we're thirsty. That way none gets spilled and no one has to mind it."

"Hmm. But what about evaporation or mosquitoes laying eggs in the water?"

Trent shrugged. "I didn't think about that. We'll drink it fast enough."

"So, use whose tarp? Yours?" Buck angled shiftily, raising his chin at Monty.

"We could play a game for it. The loser uses their tarp." Monty almost said a card game, but wasn't sure who else received cards, or whatever else wasn't promised, so he was keeping his supplies close to his chest. All he needed was to lose his life over a pack of playing cards.

"What game? I have a mean poker face," Lazarus asked with peaked interest, which answered Monty's question about the cards.

"Sure, poker, or who can toss a coconut the farthest. No matter."

"Liquor in the front, poker in the rear," Lazarus joked.

"No one's poking my rear. You know what? I can drink coconut milk. The immature ones have water inside them. I don't like the idea of sitting out in the pissing rain and getting soaked," Buck countered. "When it rains, I can open my mouth. Or I can just use my helmet and let the rain fall into it. I slept in my tarp last night and it was better in the sand than a concrete cot with no mattress back in prison. Why waste a tarp for catching water?"

"Do you think the rain will just land in your helmet or in your mouth? Sitting in the rain and getting wet isn't gonna matter if you die of thirst first." Monty laughed drily, then thought better of making Buck look foolish when Buck stared him down.

"Maybe his mouth is big enough," Lazarus added, ribbing Buck. "Or maybe he is just afraid of getting beat at poker."

"Look, we can do this solo. We may all be using our tarps if it doesn't rain enough anyway," Monty explained, dubiously scanning the sky. "We can either work together or we can stay apart. We've all got strengths and if we play to them life should be a lot simpler. Otherwise, I suppose there's one mile for each of us. We won't have to see each other." He felt irritation rising in his chest and told himself to shut up. *It's like I can't help myself from bringing up the question of how to order, or disorder, our lives.* He looked at Lazarus for his opinion.

Lazarus nodded slowly. "He's right. We need to work together. In my brotherhood we all had a job. Me and Cousin QuiQue started as lookouts, and by the end we were running the organization."

Trent added, "And if others come, like Monty said, we need to be working together to stake our claim and close ranks. If that asshole Holloman comes here, I get the first crack at him."

Monty noticed Trent tended to fall in line with whatever Lazarus wanted, a follower who picked someone to rally around.

"Monty's right," Trent continued. "Long term we'll need some sort of reservoir. We can't drink salt water. Buck, you can't drink coconut milk all the time. You'll never have a solid shit again if you drink only coconut milk. It's a laxative."

Unaccustomed to submitting to anything, Buck bridled at being led along. "Well, I wanna go exploring the rest of the island. Before you start setting up shit and building dikes and pyramids you may want to look around the place first, don't'cha think? And I don't think anyone else is coming either. We are their guinea pigs. They ain't gonna drop more guinea pigs until they finish their first lab experiment. Measure how loud we squeal. Weeee weeee weeeeeee."

And, in a way, Buck was correct.

CHAPTER 9: Trent Doyle – The Tweaker

Trent, a farm boy from Mudhole, Missouri, was the typical drug addict, who turned first to retail theft, then robbery, then mutated into a murderer. Admittedly, he had a hard start. Much of life's early possibilities were sapped out of him before he entered grade school. By the time he was six, his parents fell into alcoholism, lost their farm, and he spent many months with them on the streets living rough, impoverished, and surviving in a drainage culvert under a bridge. During the farming season, when times were good, they worked as hired hands and lived in a mobile home park. Eventually and predictably, Trent led a life similar to his parents.

In high school, his favorite thing was to spend "all tweakend long" on Desoxyn. He'd be freewheeling, Frankensteinin' (taking junk apart and putting it back together), and doing weirdly postured Chuck Norris moves. Before age twenty-five he was a frequent flyer in the criminal system, with a misdemeanor and felony list as long as his arm, exclusively for non-violent crimes involving drug possession or petty thievery from commercial establishments. At that point, his crimes could be categorized as more "need over greed" and a trickle effect of bad decisions. He graduated to cooking methamphetamine in his mobile home, but that ceased when he burned himself, requiring skin grafts sliced from his thighs and transferred to his chest.

Having no medical insurance, the resulting bills were excessive and went unpaid.

While out on parole for ten-fingering a bagel truck, he went on an epic binge. His plan was to pay off his hospital debt. Whistling like a fiend, he robbed a bank disguised in an old Daffy Duck Halloween mask and brandishing a gun. While he was jerking and twitching, a clerk triggered the silent alarm. Hopped up and nervous, his motormouth was running a mile a minute and his eyes were darting in every direction under the mask. He went behind the counter to force the tellers to access all the cash drawers. That's when the situation took a violent turn. Feeling like he could take Trent, a cowboy in line who was carrying concealed stood up quickly and went to pull his weapon but Trent beat him on the trigger—being an expert video gamer had its advantages—which resulted in a first-degree murder charge.

Alerted that hostages were in the bank, the police arrived on scene outside the building and yelled to Trent on a megaphone. The cursing, dying vigilante coughing blood and tactical team negotiations blaring on the speaker further freaked out Trent. They lobbed in a tear gas canister and he volleyed back a round of gunfire, hoping the small-town police would disperse for a minute so he could escape. One female customer, who was lying on her stomach, was accidentally killed by the return police gunfire, which resulted in an additional felony murder charge. When Trent surrendered, his goose was stuffed and cooked.

He spent ten years on death row at the SCU, dreading the lethal cocktail injection—the only chemicals he was loath to consume.

CHAPTER 10: Hot Rod Cooper

Roderick Cooper was a childhood prodigy who was working on his doctorate when other teens in high school were learning how to roll joints and smoke weed. Tested by Duke University in the eighth grade, he was found to be a genius. He graduated at the age of twenty-one with doctoral degrees in both engineering and physics, and flew through government security clearances to the highest level Q clearance.

It wasn't until he was doing projects for the Army and Air Force that he began to display symptoms of schizophrenia. It started innocuously enough: he would talk to himself and laugh. It became noticeable to others when he began carrying on private conversations, pausing as if he was listening to someone. "That's not right. That's not right," he'd mutter to the blackboard of fiddly formulas. He was working on a high-level missile guidance system when he began to hear voices. At first, Rod rationalized the chatter in his head. He told his family, who were Scientologists, he was being watched, but they assumed given his job that concept wasn't entirely out of the question. They suggested he quit his job and go in for auditing and then a purification or an introspection rundown to clear his head. He resisted. The auditory hallucinations, primarily voices, became increasingly louder, more insistent and hateful. His paranoiac thoughts were splitting and multiplying like the brooms in Disney's *The*

Sorcerer's Apprentice. By the time his paranoia became glaringly obvious to his coworkers, the light on his fuse was lit and burning to the end.

With sympathy, Rod was sent to an employee assistance program. But his security clearance was pulled and he was terminated because he became unpredictable. He refused to continue taking a psychiatrist's prescribed anti-psychotics, insisting it was "a medical straitjacket" and they were "forcing lucidity" on him. When medicated, he felt like his mind, formerly a sharp instrument, was dulled to uselessness by the chemicals. He attempted suicide and was remanded to a hospital until he was deemed to no longer be a danger to himself.

Rod was convinced the Army and the CIA were out to get him because his formulas were "too advanced" for them to understand, which his employer pointed out was patently absurd. Then, he chalked up his firing to his refusal to work on nuclear weapons and his qualms about the misappropriation of science in general. "You do bad things," he told them. Since he signed a non-compete agreement when he was initially hired that cited his "position of unique trust," he couldn't work independently or for a competitor in military, security, or intelligence for a year. He also could not publish papers in scientific journals. Hamstrung, he cocooned himself in his house, talking to himself and scrawling complex formulas all over the walls he claimed the government would love to have. He lined his windows with tinfoil to scramble any signals, and he nailed sheets on the wall over them, then comforters over that. He fashioned a Faraday cage around his bed and slept in it. Feeling they picked up better reception for spying, he pulled out two of his molars that had metal fillings, without anesthesia and by candlelight. On the mental edge, these were the kind of shenanigans that went on to which no one was privy.

After reading the news of a missile explosion in the newspaper, he went into a wilder tailspin. *They have been attempting my formulas and they don't know what they are doing!* He was convinced they had broken into his home and stolen his latest equations, which he had yet to debug and that he also wasn't putting on his computer because he was sure he was being surveilled. He left the scribbled research purposely incomplete because he insisted, "The only privacy we have is in our minds." That's when everything went haywire. He was only twenty-three years old and the voices were telling him to send a craft onto the base to stymie their efforts. They became fair game because they invaded his privacy. So, he flew a homemade drone to the server to melt it down, thereby erasing the data.

Rod guided the drone into the restricted area as easy as you please, which was laughable in itself. Formulas are not as sexy as the weapons themselves. His plan was to roast the server, thus wiping out his formulas and figuratively taking back his intellectual property. No more, no less. Rod knew who worked on what projects and on which equipment the data was stored. No one in his department worked in the wee hours of a weekend, especially not in the high-security wing of the building. The SNAFU in Rod's plan was that the server experienced a technical difficulty and tech support was sent in at 2 a.m. on that Saturday to fix the problem. One employee was hunched over the equipment and another was at a nearby terminal typing away. When the drone's camera captured the men's presence, Rod attempted to abort the mission. It failed. The base attack was captured on multiple videos. The two technical engineers and a dozing security guard in the building were blown to pieces.

Naked and afraid, Rod gave himself to the authorities. In addition to three counts of murder in the first degree, Rod was also charged with and convicted of espionage after the government found he had placed typed copies of documents they deemed classified in safe-deposit boxes in his name all around the city, along with rambling letters expressing disillusionment with the US Government. The FBI also seized documents from inside Rod's home that were neither logged nor seen again. Regardless of the murders, Rod was generally not well-known to the public. The misinformed media, who called the explosion a terrorist attack, was not corrected. The crime was Rod's first and only offense.

Taken into custody, it was patently obvious to everyone Rod was not well and not on any medication. He'd crouch in the middle of his cell rocking like a crazy person, yanking at his hair and yelling, "Make them stop screaming!" Over and over. Generous doses of Haldol and Lithium seemed to level him out long enough to hold a conversation. He told his attorney afterward, "It was like I was overhearing their evil plans. I can't hear those now. Maybe I screwed up." When off his meds, he was clearly insane and unable to be legally executed. Rod's family scolded him when they visited, pleading with him to never mention his religion, and blamed him, saying he had no business reading the newspaper that day anyway. Rod told them not to visit because he didn't want to put their lives in danger. "They will not only punish me. They'll punish those around me." Eventually, his church labeled him subversive and, after his savings ran out, his family wouldn't pay for his private attorney. The jury convicted him of three counts of murder in the first degree and five counts of espionage. His appeals were primarily based on the question of his state of mind, both during the crime and in his present state. Fine hairs were split over the legal definition of the term insanity.

After Rod stabilized, he always wanted back off the medications because he didn't like the way they made him feel sluggish, unfocused, and unable to concentrate on his formulas. He engaged in countermeasures to avoid consuming the meds, like tonguing his pills and going on starvation strikes, because he was convinced they dosed his food. For sixteen years he waited on death row as the government tried in turns to medicate him in order to kill him. One time he went catatonic for two weeks when an execution date was scheduled. At another point he was forcibly administered electroconvulsive therapy, which knocked out his underlying depression and most of the negative effects of his schizo disorder. But he was still slightly off, which resulted in continual delays in his execution date. The government's endgame was seemingly to make him well enough to be executed, with which his treating doctors did not agree. Eventually the prison became lax about medicating him, except when he was in the throes of a fit. Roderick Cooper was a bit of a legal sticky wicket. But, depositing him on an island with other murderers was considered legal and viable. Rod was the first inmate at CMU to receive the offer.

Oddly enough, the prison allowed Rod to receive monthly subscriptions to scientific magazines and journals.

CHAPTER 11: The Shittin' Place

Buck waltzed over to the lagoon, dropped his boxer shorts, and started pissing like a whale's spout. "Hey, it's Moby Dick," he drawled. His comportment, or lack thereof, set Monty's teeth on edge.

"How much water did you drink, dude?" Trent chuckled at Buck's animal display of bravado. "Be careful. Something might bite that thing off."

Buck leered. "They are watching my johnson from space. Right, Hot Rod?"

"Nasty," Monty commented.

"Don't start giving me a morality lecture," Buck replied.

Lazarus wasn't amused. "Don't shit or piss where you eat. That's basic. That's just common decency. Do it away from the Blue Lagoon and don't do it at The Drop either." Since there were no streets or paths, they started naming the natural landmarks.

"Speaking of which, we could make a latrine or something nearby. You know, dig a ditch, make planks, and hang our asses over. Use leaves as toilet paper and all that," Monty suggested to Lazarus. Monty had previously considered these creature comforts and other necessities, but was reluctant to broach the subject to the group after Buck's initial truculence.

Still urinating, Buck responded over his shoulder. "How are we gonna dig a latrine, old soldier? The soil is shit here. Haven't you noticed?"

"If we want a main camp we should clean up an area," Lazarus replied, picking up Monty's idea.

Monty was relieved. *Let Lazarus take the lead and be the shot caller. Let him have the bull's-eye on his back when someone gets rubbed wrong.*

"I was homeless before. I can help," Trent quickly offered. He embarked on a long-winded narrative about his harrowing early life on the streets. As he was accustomed to grinding poverty and living in the wild, Trent's opinion carried weight. "In the 'burbs you can't even wander into the woods without running across a random toilet and dumped roof tiles. I wish we had some of that. Let's look for trash on the shore because I can construct shit. Taking stuff apart and putting it back together was my thing for years and years. The island has almost everything we need for basic shelter. First, let's keep camp away from the jungle. It's chock full of mosquitoes. I couldn't sleep last night for swatting them. The closer to the shore and the wind the better. But let's mark the high tide to make sure we clear the water."

"There's some old driftwood down past The Drop we could use as benches," Monty ventured with a fake shrug while his mind was busy strategizing. "And we can scavenge our parachutes to construct the buildings."

"Aren't you three full of ideas," Buck jeered, tucking his junk back in his shorts. "We are free from rules now. And I don't feel like doing any extra shit. Let's quit candy-coating our words. I'm exploring tomorrow."

"Suit yourself. But we have all the time in the world to explore," Monty said.

"We have all the time in the world to construct a camp, too. If we're all gonna die here anyway, why not have some fun first?" Buck threw a rock into the lagoon and viewed the ripples through his half-masted lids.

Lazarus voiced the words Monty was thinking. "You wanna hang at the camp, then you gotta help, know what I mean?" Lazarus pointed a friendly yet rebuking finger. "And I want an ocean view. Let's make camp near The Drop."

Pursing his lips, Monty tried mightily to not make plain his lack of affection for Buck. "So, you don't want a camp, I take it?" he asked Buck.

"Take it however you please. How are you gonna know where the best place is if you don't explore?" Buck sallied. "Since you are so sure others might come, don't you think we should find and secure the best, most ad-van-tageous spot?" Buck ridiculed Monty's fancy speech. "Until then I can just roll up in my tarp or find a cave."

"There are no caves on this atoll," Monty bluntly corrected him.

"So you don't believe in doing things or-gan-ic-ally, letting things develop as they do?" Buck mocked.

"Of course I do."

Trent interrupted their banter. "So, should camp be at The Drop or here at Blue Lagoon? It's windier at The Drop so there's less mosquitoes."

"The wood and supplies are better here at Blue Lagoon. There are more resources. It's less noisy. It's calmer and surely it's got better fishing than The Drop," Monty said.

"The drones have an unrestricted view at the beachline," Rod added. "There's denser tree cover at Blue Lagoon, for what it's worth. But they can still see everything with infrared."

"Two for The Drop, two for Blue Lagoon. Are you gonna have five ideas on how to do everything to break a tie?" Buck said.

The conversation inevitably circled back to the cannibal. Buck laughed sharply. "If you set up camp right at The Drop, he's gonna know exactly where you might be."

Trent suggested coupling into partners and creating a comfort zone. "Well, there's five of us and one of him. Wherever we go, we should team up and use the buddy system. If we're sleeping side-by-side or near each other, we can band together if he or anybody else comes. Me and Laz can crash together."

"Good idea, son," Lazarus approved. "Quien a buen arbol se arrima, buena sombra lo cobija." (Which meant he who takes shelter under a good tree gets the best shade.)

"Thinning out nearby trees around us will make it so he can't sneak up on us," Monty mused. "And lighting torches at intervals so we're not sitting around the campfire with him behind us lurking in the bushes."

"He'll have less hiding space at The Drop," Trent said.

"The Drop it is," Lazarus decreed. "And we find that cannibal before he finds us."

"What are we gonna do to the cannibal?" Monty said. "Shoot him with air pistols? While we'd be less scared if he wasn't around anymore, if we did something to him wouldn't we feel dirty again?"

"Scared? Speak for yourself. I'm not scared of that fuckin' cannibal." Buck licked his lips and swallowed hard. He postured, perfecting his thousand-yard stare.

Monty found Buck more unlikeable as the hours ticked by. He questioned everyone and relished pointing out errors. Even Buck's lanky ponytail annoyed him. Buck's receding hairline at his temples was so sharp it looked like horns. The thing that chafed Monty the most was Buck's lack of discipline.

Around the bright flickering fire back at The Drop, Monty noticed an eerie stillness and an unnerving feeling of being watched. Or maybe it was all the continual discussion about the cannibal and his predatory instincts. In the dark, the fire's light flared their faces in a ghoulish manner. It also peopled the beach with shadow figures that danced—sometimes jumping, sometimes hunching, but always moving.

CHAPTER 12: Order in Paradise

Everyone tended to wake early, and developed his own routine. Lazarus and Trent went running along the beach, enjoying the physical motion. Monty liked to do his business in peace. Being able to use the bathroom unobserved was a simple pleasure. Afterward, Monty found Buck on the beach playing like a child, mounding sand and digging a trench around it.

Monty laughed. "What the heck are you doing?"

"What does it look like I'm doing?" Buck replied.

"It appears you are building a sandcastle, complete with a moat." Monty failed to hide his amusement.

"I've never built one before. Not everyone lived on a beach."

"Carry on, then. Carry on." Monty reproached himself for goading Buck, but shook his head at the idea of crafting castles made of sand without having a real sleeping structure.

To clear The Drop for camp they first needed to remove all the accumulated debris, consisting of profuse amounts of empty shells, coconut husks, dead rotten limbs, seaweed, and trash, mostly plastic bottles. They put the bottles in a pile with the hope of eventually filling them with rainwater. Rod was preoccupied with the refuse, excited every time they discovered a soda can, and declared with a glimmer in his eye that he would "make a surprise" out of them.

They opted for Trent's method of fashioning temporary sleeping structures. "We don't need headroom, just sleeping room." He suggested they erect pup tents with the Pisonia branches broken as evenly as possible and lashed together with vines. He stated that using palm fronds for roofing and then draping their blue tarps over the structures would keep out both the rain and mosquitoes. They chose large fronds, ripped them down the middle, and stacked them horizontally like roof tiles. His method of using one tarp on top would still leave the moist sand exposed, so the act of bunking up in pairs and using the other man's tarp to line the flooring would feasibly keep two men dry in about six by ten feet of slanted space. For added comfort and insulation, they lined the floor with layers of fronds and seaweed. Trent said that later on they could make more permanent structures up on stilts. Since Trent already bonded with Lazarus, Monty was paired with Rod by default. Buck made it abundantly clear he wanted no part in a sleeping tent and continued crafting his fortified sandcastle, the only structure he felt like fashioning. Since Rod had offered his tarp for use as water catcher, Monty's tent was lined on the bottom with his parachute. Even though the tents were situated under some branches for shade, they opened the tents at the sides to allow air to pass through, otherwise the temperature inside would roast in the daytime and be stifling in the evenings. Monty draped his mosquito net over the tent's front flap. The camp was hedged by trees to its north, the sea to its south, and beachfront to its east and west. They thought about erecting a thorn wall at the edges of camp in the future, a barrier of spikes like those found in Africa to keep lions at bay. Not for lions, but the cannibal or any newcomers. Good solid wood would need to be found and sharpened to a point.

While scavenging for materials, Rod kept insisting he could make something out of a drone if they could capture one. "We can use it against them." He spoke repeatedly about drones and spying.

"Shut up about the damn drones unless you can make us an aircraft to fly away," Buck barked testily from the shore as he filled the moat around his castle with seawater.

Taking a good five steps back, Rod squealed in meek surprise. "Don't snap at me!"

Monty called Rod over. He perked up at Trent's idea of weaving the palm fronds to create other objects. "If we pick long and thin ones we can weave them together over and under style, like baskets. And we can make hats too!" Trent got Rod and Monty so invested in the idea of various patterns that Buck joked, "You all sound like a bunch of grandmas or old-maidish aunts in a sewing circle."

Monty surveyed the campsite. It'd been built with breezy speed. It didn't even take them a day to erect their structures. Though Buck had declared he was going to spend the afternoon exploring, Monty noticed he waited until the others were finished to look around the island with them. They were also on the lookout for the cannibal—some guided by habit, some guided by greed, some guided by fear.

Following the cries of the din of terns, they found smelly Birds' Nest, as they came to name it, and all its accumulated guano. The area was a vast section of weather-worn lava rock with many pits and very shallow pools where hundreds of birds had set up a colony.

Buck said, "Imagine that. Little pools of water ready for the drinking. No need for a tarp contraption."

"If you want to sip bird-shit water, then knock yourself out," Trent stated. "Go for it. I dare you."

Lazarus laughed. "Little pools of chicken shit."

Buck didn't drink any.

They discovered that egg raiding at Birds' Nest offered the quickest food source, as the egg-filled nests were built on the ground and the birds didn't do much to fight off interlopers. The eggs were ripe for the picking. While they tasted sort of fishy, they cooked easily on the hot rock. Lazarus also collected the abandoned eggshells.

That night's dinner consisted of crab, egg, and Trent introduced the men to island salad made from the starchy hearts of palms. He showed them that by peeling off the outer layer of the stalk of a budding palm, cracking it open, and then peeling it back like celery, the middle was both edible and sweet. He warned, however, that eating it destroyed the entire plant. Over the meal, Monty made a toast with coconut milk. "To Island X. Look at that view!"

The island was heightening Monty's senses of taste, sight, smell, and sound. That evening around their new structures the sky was aflame in an otherworldly hue. When the fiery red sunset, a vivid crimson shading into scarlet, loomed on the horizon every man was awed into silence. Except Rod, who hopped up on a lava rock and declared a premonition. "It's a bad color. I feel doom because I see blood, blood, and more blood. Bubbles of blood!" He ran his fingers in his hair until it was wild and then made circling hand gestures in the air. "Can't you see it? Evil in the clouds, too!"

"Enough with that crazy talk." Lazarus scolded him lightly, but added, "We should definitely stay together until we know where that cannibal is at."

Chastised, Rod ducked his head. Just when they weren't thinking about the cannibal, something like the sunset would reignite their contagious fear.

In their newly erected tent, Monty tried sleeping head to foot with the wiggly Rod, who rolled around too much on the dried fronds for Monty's liking. Monty waited behind closed eyelids for sleep to come. Though Rod was small in stature and took up little space, Monty still felt uncomfortable. Trying not to think about his previous life, Monty reviewed his preconceived notions of the other men. Lazarus was a curious mixture of joviality and ruthlessness. He was emerging as the leader, but open to suggestion. Trent was helpful, knowledgeable about survival, and partial to Lazarus. Rod was both highly intelligent and high-strung. Monty and Rod had a shared interest in aviation. For Buck he felt repugnance. He was lazy, crass, and combative. He acted like he'd never received any tenderness in this world. Buck had done nothing to better Monty's original opinion. Monty resolved to tolerate him as best he could.

He wondered what these men would do in a crisis. What if the cannibal struck their camp in the dead of night? Monty's own habit was to black out. He doubted Rod would be the hero.

As the hours ticked by, Monty realized he didn't mind Rod's company. In fact, he was comforted by his proximity when an extremely noisy wind from out of nowhere picked up and sounded like the rattle of dry bones. A soft patter of rain quickly turned into a torrential downpour accompanied by a sideways slanted wind. Thankfully, their tent proved tight, and Monty sighed in relief that their water catcher would be brimming with fresh drinking water. Finally Monty dozed, but he slept badly. Both he and Rod awoke to a shriek coming from the other structure.

"What the hell is that?" Monty heard the thudding sound of skin on skin as Lazarus yelped, punched out and hit Trent, who was the closest body to him inside their tent.

"Ouch! Dude, you punched me. What are you doing?" Trent yelled in pain, surprise, and confusion.

"What was that? Something ran across my face. It was all warm and the size of a cat," Lazarus shouted. He and Trent hustled out of their tent so fast the makeshift structure tottered sideways.

Rain dripping down his neck, Trent peeked in warily. "I think there's a rat in there. You didn't have to hit me, Lazarus." He rubbed his shoulder where the blow had landed.

They stood in the dark pouring rain looking dumbly at the ramshackle structure. All except Buck, who was wrapped up like a burrito in his tarp and peeked his head out at the first noise. He found it all quite amusing. "You had company and didn't know it."

Wild scrabbling and squealing issued from inside Lazarus and Trent's tent.

"I hate those rata, alimañas." Lazarus shuddered. "I can take a lot of shit, but not rata. No mas rata. Those motherfuckers bite. My cousin QuiQue got bit on the cheek once. Someone kill it."

Buck smacked his hands, clapping them together once loudly, and Lazarus jumped.

Rod gently stepped forward. "It just wants out of the rain. It hasn't learned to be wary of people. You scared it." He lifted up the corner of the blue tarp.

"Hey there. Hey," he whispered. The sleek rat scurried into the darkness.

Lazarus moved back and forth on his feet like a restless elephant and wiped his face repeatedly. "This sleeping is shit. I got jitters now. Don't know if they good jitters or bad jitters. We need a lookout."

"For rats?" Buck sniggered and ducked back into his tarp to sleep.

"I'll watch out," Rod offered. "I really don't sleep much anyway." In the drizzle, wrapped in a portion of his parachute, he took position on the highest lava rock, a mere three feet off the ground, near the shore while Lazarus and Trent crawled back into their semi-collapsed tent.

As the others slept, Rod kept vigil over everyone's fears.

CHAPTER 13: Montgomery "Monty" Davenport, III

Monty was known in the Florida headlines as the Ice Pick Murderer. A model inmate during his twenty-year stint on death row, at fifty years old he is the oldest man on Island X. Monty was convicted of the slaughter of his wife and two undercover federal agents in an "orgy of drugs and murder" at his Palm Beach mansion.

Some memories Monty lived over and over, yet about the most important, the most life changing, he had no recall. Monty couldn't tell anyone what happened that night in 1996. He never claimed to be a choirboy, but his accused crimes were unspeakable. He awoke that January morning on the brown sectional couch in his living room to pure horror. The television was blaring a cartoon, *The Bugs Bunny and Tweety Show*. His daughter, Chelsea, was annoyingly tapping his forehead. Blinking slowly, he thought, *I'm still dreaming or she got into the refrigerator again. Dammit.* Ketchup was everywhere. He opened one red, bleary eye. What a mess. On her hands. On her face. In her ears, where she'd tucked back her blonde hair.

"Daddy, get up. Mommy hasn't fixed breakfast. She has a boo-boo. See?"

Chelsea shoved her fingers in his face and he smelled the tang of coppery blood.

"Holy shit," he strangled out, shoving himself up and fully awake. He rubbed his eyes and refocused. His wife, sprawled on the sectional at his feet, was a bloody mess. Her dress, white last night, appeared red. She had removed her shoes in order to discretely access a vein in her foot, her favorite shooting spot. The works were still in an open cigar box on the coffee table: syringes, spoons, cotton, and lighters. An empty highball glass sat beside a water-filled ice bucket. Weekend fun. Chipping. But something entirely different did her in. An ice pick protruded jauntily from her long, delicate throat. His daughter, crawling over him and then to his wife, flicked the weapon's handle.

"See? Mommy can't talk. Everyone is sleeping. I'm hungry."

"Oh, shit! Oh, shiiyiiit!" It was his new mantra. The ice pick had been a present and a running joke. Every time his uncle, the former senator, came to their house and drank his scotch on the rocks he laughed at the "bourgeois" large ice cubes Monty served from his refrigerator. Bobby preferred chipped ice. "Have Rosalita come here and crush some, for God's sake."

"I don't have a Rosalita," Monty poked back. His uncle's Christmas present to Monty that year was the ice pick, decorated with the gayest bow ever, and a personal check. *Now, hire a Rosalita*, the accompanying card read. But Monty never hired a maid or a housekeeper.

The dealer and his friend, clad in polo shirts and faded madras shorts, were kicked back in the La-Z-Boy recliners nearby. Also splattered in "ketchup."

Monty panicked. How an ice pick came to be lodged almost up to its handle in his wife's neck was a mystery. The dead men, one still with the needle dangling out of his arm, were equally ladled in blood.

He grabbed Chelsea into his arms, startling her, and skidded to the powder room off the immense foyer, putting her inside her time-out spot. He had to get her away from the scene, look around, and try to think. Hearing the door shut, she screamed in anger at him. "Doody-head," she yelled. "I'm hungry!"

"It's okay, honey. Daddy's just playing. You stay in there. Give me one minute," he called back, voice shaking. "Daddy's losing his mind," he mumbled hoarsely. He ran through the house, peeping around doors, looking in closets, and squinting under beds, searching for intruders but found no one.

Heading back to the foyer, he saw Chelsea poke her little fingers under the door. "Daddy, let me out," she whined. "Nowwww." He saw his own hands were clean.

"Oh, shit." Monty ran his fingers through his thick hair. Looking around he saw Chelsea must have wandered around awhile. Her tiny, bloody footprints marked the terra cotta tile. His size eleven prints now intermixed with hers.

This isn't happening. I have to call 911. But I can't leave the drugs here. I could flush them. He thought as he paced. His mind whirled in panic mode. *No. If I hide the works, there is still a needle hanging out of this dude's arm. Oh, and an ice pick in Angela's neck. They're dead. My wife is dead. There's nothing I can do for them.* He caught a look at himself in one of the large gilt mirrors and saw a spooked George Clooney look-a-like staring back. *Beat it. Now. What are you waiting for,* he imagined it replied. He took the advice.

Monty opened the bathroom door and snatched up Chelsea, who brightened at the attention. He hustled to her bedroom, stripped off her *Rugrats* pajamas in a wad and quickly wiped her face and hands with them. He put on her favorite matching clothes. Running with her on his hip to the master bedroom, he changed as she waited, whistling, for him on the California King bed. Dashing them back to the foyer, he grabbed the Porsche keys from a brass wall hanger shaped like a sailboat. Seeing they were going somewhere, Chelsea cried out, "Bumbles! Don't forget Mr. Bumbles!" Bumbles was the cheap, stuffed bumblebee he won for her at the fair. He ran back into her room scouring for Bumbles. Jumping in the Porsche, the garage door couldn't open fast enough and he almost plowed into it as he reversed. "We're going to Uncle Bobby's. Don't you wanna see Uncle Bobby?" he chattered madly.

"I'm hungry," she declared.

"You can have Cheerios at Uncle Bobby's."

As he raced along, he caught a look at Chelsea with her hand out the rolled down window making Bumbles rise up and down, flying in the wind. Smeared blood was still behind her ear and in her hair. He sped to his uncle's house, who, to add insult to injury, wasn't even home. His housekeeper said the senator had taken his yacht, Just Us Buoys, out on the open sea for "a fortnight." Monty, utterly dazed, accompanied by his attorney, turned himself in for questioning that evening, was arrested and arraigned the next day, and denied bail.

The evidence against Monty was buttoned up tighter than his attorney's three-piece suit, with no loose ends in sight. No reasonable doubt questions existed without plausible alternatives. The coroner's report read that all the victims died from near-lethal dosages of heroin, accompanied by an ice pick rampage. The bodies, riddled with holes, spoke to a rage killing, a triple execution. The household ice pick was simply a weapon of opportunity. The DNA on and in their wounds told the order of the murders. The men were stabbed first, then his wife. The wound pathology of near-perfect circles left by the ice pick in their flesh showed also that the victims did not move to defend themselves. It was overkill and appeared personal. There was no forced entry to the mansion and no unaccounted for fingerprints.

Monty's prior criminal record consisted of merely a dinky marijuana possession charge from his first year of college. The federal government offered him life imprisonment without parole for a guilty plea to three counts of first-degree murder, which he refused. The case went to trial. The government's narrative became the story. The residents of Palm Beach didn't want to believe a crazed killer was on the loose. The prosecution invented a lurid tale of jealousy, divorce, and an impending drug bust, claiming that Monty discovered Angela was having an affair with one of the agents and fixing to set Monty up and he snapped. The fact Monty claimed he could remember none of it was either false or convenient they insisted. The feds went as far as putting an expert on the stand who implied the use of an ice pick was an obvious phallic substitute, which elicited one of the only occasions where the gallery chuckled. His defense mitigation specialist attempted to humanize Monty to no avail. The mitigating characteristics were numerous: Monty had a college degree, worked for Habitat for Humanity, sat on many boards, and helped various political campaigns. But the gruesome crime scene photos told another story. They showed the actions of a madman, with the blood spatter on the walls tossed up to the ceiling and drugs lying around while his daughter presumably slept unattended. The bloody footprint pictures made the news.

After Monty's arrest, Chelsea was allowed to live with Bobby, his wife, and his older children. Monty's parents had passed years before in a car accident, and Bobby had also raised him. As Monty came from a multi-generational political family, some politicians capitalized on Monty's crime and used it to defame his extended family. Many in the opposition did the victory dance behind closed doors. Strangely, all the Freedom of Information Act requests by

Monty's attorney concerning the undercover agents were denied. It was long after his first trial that Monty realized he was a convict. The improbable title of murderer simply did not adhere to him.

In 2014, testing revealed foreign DNA at the scene, but the government argued it could have come from anyone, even a criminalist. Monty was denied a third appeal. He lasted twenty years on the death row simply because he had the best attorneys money could buy and they kept the semi-effective appeals process going. Since that day in 1996 when he awoke to a bloodbath, Monty's dreams, when he does sleep, are plagued with nightmares and confusion. In his fevered rest he can never wipe all the blood from Chelsea's face no matter how many handkerchiefs or T-shirts he uses. *But my hands were clean.*

CHAPTER 14: Inherent Dangers

The island had a rhythm like a song: the crashing of surf-beat, birds squawking in the afternoon, whispering breezes, rain pattering at night. The buzzing insects constructed and deconstructed in a hypnotic cycle of birth, death, and rebirth. The circle of life was right before Monty's eyes, all of their eyes, if they cared to look. The clouds were alive with movement, shape-shifting.

Monty enjoyed watching the different breeds of seabirds interact. They attempted to one-up each other with their caws, shooting lordly looks. He was fascinated by the way they dried themselves on the branches with their wings outstretched or all stood facing the same direction in the wind.

Rod took to talking to the plants and trees, communing with them. They responded by flourishing.

The crab proved so abundant and easy to catch that, coupled with the eggs they harvested, they hadn't yet attempted fishing or prospecting the rest of the atoll. "A man needs like 1,400 calories every single day just to stay functioning," Trent jabbered. "That's a lot of egg, crab and coconut. Let's find something different."

That morning, the lagoon's reef was crystal clear and transparent. Monty could see straight to the bottom. "It's like a fish tank. I can see every detail."

Eagerly, he jumped in the shallower section of the neck-deep lagoon, flopping and washing himself. The others, except Rod, joined in. Dry above his calves, Rod, who couldn't swim, drew water into a coconut half-shell and commenced a bird bath on the shore.

Everything was quite lovely until Rod squealed, "Shark! Shark! Shaaark!" He pointed and waved his long, white fingers, at which Trent, Lazarus, and Monty hurled themselves out of the water. Buck, playing it too cool for school, ignored the watery stampede and floated on his back, slowly kicking his feet like a Mississippi riverboat. The fast-moving shark came right at him, swung around, and nipped his foot.

"Whoa!" he yelped with a jerk when his right foot was snagged by the glancing bite. He hauled himself out of the lagoon holding his bleeding appendage, which at worst may have required a few stitches. The dripping blood quickly attracted more sharks to the scene. Their black tips circled the area with expectation. "Where did those mothers come from?"

Monty regarded Buck in baffled wonderment. "Didn't you hear Rod? Why didn't you get out? When you splash around like that sharks think you are wounded, fish food. It's like waving meat in front of their noses. That was reckless."

"How do I know what he is or isn't seeing with his wild imagination and not just being crazy?" Buck snapped in anger, pointing at Rod.

In a hurt tone, Rod stated the obvious. "I told you a shark was coming and it bit you. Now you're bleeding."

Lazarus looked at the wound. "You may want to clean that out with alcohol wipes and put on your socks or flops so that don't get infected until it heals."

Buck whined like a petulant child. "Son-of-a-bitch shark!" He couldn't have been that badly pained because he had enough energy to snatch up and spitefully throw a couple of shells, rocks, and blistering invectives at the sharks, but the sly creatures swam off as fast as they'd arrived. Buck resumed his self-pitying moans. He held his toe tightly until the bleeding slowed, cursing all the while.

"Stop chirpin'. You think cavemen whined?" Lazarus scolded.

Buck slung off his bandana and tied it around his foot. Trent helped him hop back to camp. "Put your arm around me but take it easy, my back is sunburned. Next time you swim take a stick with you and poke 'em in the nose or eye," Trent advised as he trudged along with Buck.

The rest of the group gingerly explored the shallow reefs as the sun dried their bodies. In addition to sharks teeming all around, sea urchins, moray eels, and stingrays were the next obvious dangers. Had they spent time looking before leaping deeper into the lagoon, they would have seen the harm lurking beneath the surface. They would have seen that the terrain was wild and rugged like them.

"There's danger in there," Rod spoke quietly.

"We have to be careful about which fish we eat, too. Some of these may be poisonous," Monty mentioned. After the calamity with Buck, Monty was in no mood for another fiasco.

Lazarus nodded knowingly. "Ciguatera."

"Cigar-what?" Rod tried to guess at Lazarus's Spanish.

"No. Ciguatera poison. The algae that grows on the coral here is malo, bad. Certain fish eat it. And if you eat those fish you will croak," Lazarus explained. "And never eat the fish's head."

"Well, fishing out in the sea and not here in the lagoon should offer a better chance of avoiding the poison," Monty reckoned. "Only certain fish are susceptible to it, like the red snapper. When we fish here, we can use a fishing pole or a spear. We could stay up on shore and not even risk shark bite. Or maybe we can make a raft and use a mosquito net to gather them."

"Make a jetty. That's the answer," Lazarus said.

"I know aeronautics. I can make a spear that'll fly far and fast," Rod offered. "It's just engineering and physics."

"Or a bent needle from our sewing kit can act as a fishing hook," Monty suggested. "Why else did they give us needles? To stitch up Buck's wounds?" Monty snorted dismissively.

"Aw, son." Lazarus slapped his thighs. "We can use needles to make tattoos. Hey, what should our island symbol be? Since this is Island X, the tat could be an island shape or a horseshoe shape with a big black X over it."

"Tattoos? But how?" Rod wondered.

Lazarus rubbed his hands together. "You leave it to me. My cousin was a master tat artist. Charcoal makes the best black ink."

"What about your brotherhood and your cousin? Do you think any of them may get dropped here to join us?" Rod asked.

"Nah, they are in the state pen. I was the only one left on death row." Lazarus appeared solemn. "They already killed my cousin, QuiQue, Jose Guerrero. They put him at Supermax so we wouldn't be together and take over."

"QuiQue, that's a funny name."

Lazarus crossed himself. "God rest his soul. He tried to take all the blame and the rap. He said he did it alone. He tried to save me."

"We can be your family now," Rod said.

CHAPTER 15: The Cannibal

Hans Fritzl, or as his mother called him, Hansi, was convicted of multiple murders and hate crimes. Throughout his life, Jewish girls, and then women, within a certain proximity to Hansi Fritzl seemed to go mysteriously missing.

Hans, a strapping 6'2" Nordic-Aryan looking mensch, was born and bred in California. He was the only child of German-American parents who hailed from the German city of Essen. Very early on, Hans sensed he was different from the other kids, and not just by his early accented English. The first time Hansi came home singing "The Dreidel Song" the school chorus taught as a lead-up to Chanukah and Christmas, he knew he'd stepped out of line. "Das ist verboten," his angry Mutti, Elfriede, declared while furiously beating him with a wooden spoon. Hansi, an only child, was slow to catch the indoctrination of his virulently anti-Semitic parents.

On another occasion when he unwittingly tossed a bag of Lender's bagels in the shopping cart, his mother shrieked and tossed them back onto the shelf like they were on fire. Later, his father, with a disparaging look, questioned his parentage, which only incited his dominating Mutti's further rages about "Judes" and Hansi's strange fondness for them and things of their ilk.

Even in his kindergarten years, Hans had a stubborn streak in him a mile wide earning him the nickname Sturkopf, which means stubborn. For example, his Mutti always made him eat everything on his plate, even things he hated. Food and his Mutti at the dinner table were always a battleground, one he seldom won because she'd starve him out if he didn't finish his mashed turnips. Since they lived in a diverse community, his mother also set about to teach him failsafe ways of detecting Jews wherever they could be hiding so that he could strenuously avoid them. But he didn't. His parents kept him away from other children as much as possible to keep foreign influences at bay.

Our secrets make us sick.

What first made Hansi sick was little doe-eyed Hannah Lore. He lured her after school with a handpicked flower into the nearby woods, kissed her on the cheek, which she allowed, and then strangled her, which she didn't allow. The killing was spontaneous. Her murder was blamed on a homeless man who squatted in the area and had no alibi.

Hannah was his first, until high school. He had an irresistible compulsion to observe the activities of any Jewess, especially the pretty ones. His mother always insisted they did sly and tricky things, although Hans never observed any nefarious doings. The more he watched, the more he liked. The more he liked, the more he planned. The ones who spoke Yiddish remind him of his mother tongue, as it was the closest sound to the German language. The girls became "projects" for him as he trolled around stalking them. He quickly became overwhelmed by his obsessions and compulsions. If he could get them alone, he killed them. He told no one. Since Hans's parents allowed him to drink beer at mealtimes, their permissiveness set the stage for him to become an early alcoholic. And eventually, the alcohol also lessened his inhibitions, making him all the more perverse and dangerous.

Once they were dead, Hans felt nothing more for his prey. Initially, getting rid of a body was nothing but a hassle for Hans. It held no more excitement for him than an empty potato chip bag. Like the body of little Hannah Lore, he dumped them randomly at separate intervals—in woods, in the desert, in the ocean forevermore. It was the hunt and chase that pumped his adrenaline, not body disposal. After he got his driver's license and a sturdy little Volkswagen, he would cross into other counties to thwart future investigations. Once Hans lived alone and had his own place, he had even more options.

The concept of eating the bodies began with Hansi's changeling fantasy. *Am I really Aryan? Perhaps Vati was right. Perhaps I am a Jew at heart. Why else would no other women fascinate me? What if they were always inside of me?* He tentatively started his post-mortem butchery with a slab of one victim's buttock, pounded thin, breaded, seasoned and fried up like a schnitzel. He found it too chewy, so he settled on making meatballs and sausages. He chose select pieces, based upon their body types, and dumped the rest unceremoniously.

The level of control he felt afterward was simply immense and intensified, Godlike and unlike anything he'd ever experienced. He especially enjoyed dining privately on a sweetbread right before arriving for the obligatory Christmas or Easter family dinner and then declaring, "Oh, I'm too full," to his frowning mother's chagrin. *If only Mutti knew…*

When he wasn't killing, Hans felt like he was on remote control. As he was polite and respectful to those in authority, a rather quiet, banal figure, he aroused no suspicion. No one suspected Hans's murderous perversity. But underneath his slick, varnished exterior he was a chip off the old block, and those parents were two rotten planks of wood who failed to own the part they played in Hans's development.

He was twenty-six years old when he was finally caught speeding in the VW with a body in the backseat. DNA tests on the grisly frozen flesh and organs in his freezer yielded eight known victims— only a handful of those he'd slaughtered. His parents fled the country to the wilds of Argentina, more out of fear than shame. His serial murders were considered hate crimes, thus qualifying him for the federal system. His succession of attorneys were all public defenders, even one brave and hardy Jewish man named Jacob Rubenstein. Old Rubie did the best he could. After only twelve years on death row, Hans's clock was ticking out. It wasn't until he was incarcerated that he was able to gain any insight into his acts. The families of missing girls and women from miles around were dying to know where the remainder (the bones) of their relatives were for some semblance of a final burial before Hans was snuffed out. But he wasn't talking. The subtle, and not so subtle, intimidation he received in the penitentiary didn't loosen his tongue.

CHAPTER 16: The Marking

The men found getting things done in the morning, before the sun was at its hottest, was easiest. During the day, they took to going around shirtless and wearing only boxer shorts. Except Trent, who wore both his shirt and pants because he continued to be plagued by pests.

"What are we gonna do for fun? All work and no play, ya know," Trent said.

"Isn't this the point in the story when the inmates make chess figures out of soap?" Monty joked.

"Chess? More like Chinese checkers," Lazarus said. "It's rec time." He danced around on the balls of his feet. "What we gonna do?"

"Recreation time. I almost forgot what that was. Unlike the state pen, we never had real rec time at SCU, and what we did have was under armed supervision. What a joke." Trent was sunburned and, as was his manner, took to picking off his freshly peeling skin.

"I know! It's tattoo time," Lazarus crowed. He swelled with pride as he told them how his cousin QuiQue could make natural tattoos. Lazarus demonstrated. He started by gathering the coal and ashes from the dwindling fire. He placed a handful in a coconut bowl and ground it smooth with a rock in the manner of a mortar and pestle, mixing in a few drops of lagoon water until it was sticky. This black concoction was to serve as ink. Lazarus then firmly wedged one of the sewing needles into a nine-inch stick. This device was to be the tattoo gun. He dipped the needle in the ink, then used another small hard stick to tap against the improvised tattoo gun. By placing the tattoo needle against the skin and tapping the sticks together the needle pushed under the dermis leaving a tiny black dot. With repeated dippings and tappings, scoring the skin thousands of times, eventually a design emerged: a crude horseshoe covered by an X.

Rod voiced his stuttering misgivings. "I'll only get a t-tattoo if you all dig out your microchips."

Buck rolled his eyes. "Here we go. What microchip?"

"The ones in your bodies," Rod replied.

"Prove it," Trent insisted, brandishing his arm. "Find one."

Rod felt Trent's shoulder, his fingers crawling like white spiders. "This is where you received your shots, right? Initially, the government started by using electrodes in people's brains. Then this technology was created and it was a boon. Usually they'd put this kind of human microchip in your hands, but they didn't want us to notice." He poked, prodded, and ran his fingers along Trent's muscles. "Yes, yes, I think I feel it." He began pinching and kneading. "It's right here. Can you feel that tiny lump?"

"What is that?" Trent wondered as he inspected the area. "Yeah, actually, I do feel something right under the skin."

Using a shard of a broken bottle as a knife, sterilized first with an alcohol wipe, Rod dug out from under the skin a small oblong item smaller than a rice kernel. "There! That's a radiofrequency identifier microchip. Keep the correct enemy in your sight," he said as he handed over the bloody capsule.

"Well, I'll be damned!" Trent grimaced. "I thought you were full of shit."

The shaken men helped each other excise the microchips from their bodies.

Rod said, "You all probably don't wanna hear this, but electromagnetic sounds and signals are masked, hidden, in urban noise just at the threshold of your hearing. It's another way to control people. In a way, we are harder to control now that we're back in nature and away from the mainland."

Lazarus was ready to tattoo the others. Trent was his first customer, Buck second, Monty third, and Rod was last. After the first hundred or so taps, Monty felt the pain was hypnotic. A reluctant Rod winced with every puncture.

"Tough it out," Lazarus chided him at his reluctance to get his first tattoo. "What we gonna do wit you? You dug a chip out your own shoulder."

Having watched Lazarus tattoo the others, Trent marked Lazarus. Afterward, the men individually felt the ritual had bonded them on a deeper level, but they all kept it to themselves.

CHAPTER 17: Night Watch

With vigorous daily physical exercise Monty should have slept like a dead pharaoh, but instead he found himself waking and joining Rod on his night watch and having discussions. Monty found he had much in common with Rod, who was quite companionable when not manic. With no electric light, the island offered a brilliant view of the universe on cloudless evenings.

"The moon is clear," Monty said.

Rod began pointing out the galaxies. "Look at them. Have you ever seen the stars brighter? It's like viewing them with new eyes."

"They are quite amazing," Monty agreed.

"There's nothing to compete with their light. We are seeing their undiluted intensity. And it's beautiful."

"That it is," Monty said. "Seen anything else flying around?"

"Drones. They've made them solar now. And I've seen one F-22 Raptor in the daytime. They fly half the speed of sound. Not only are they stealth, they can carry heat-seeking missiles. They wanted it to be seen."

"If I don't start getting some proper sleep, I'm going to be seeing shit, too." Monty yawned.

"No, I'm actually seeing them. You can tell when I'm hallucinating because my pupils dilate."

"Oh, really? That's good to know," Monty said.

"Doctors diagnosed me with schizophrenia, paranoid schizophrenia. But I couldn't be sane or they would have executed me," Rod explained. "They wanted to kill me."

"They wanted to kill us all. So, were you faking it?"

"Oh, no, no. I just could never be completely better or I would be dead. My parents were Scientologists. My mother and sister still are. They don't believe in psychotherapy, psychiatrists, or drugs. They say drugs and toxins are stored in the body's fatty tissue. I don't know if they are wrong. I always had my own ideas about science and religion. Sometimes, when a final mystery is unfolded and you've pulled back layers and layers, you see it is a bunch of gibberish."

Unsure how to respond to Rod's frankness, Monty changed the subject. "Rod, back to the weapons. Why would they put us here just to turn around and bomb us?"

"I don't know. I am just telling you what I saw. I can tell which craft have payload because I know their design. Maybe they don't want us trying to escape. Maybe it's just a reminder." Rod paused. "We've been away from civilization for five days. I've had quite a lot of time to really think."

Monty chuckled. "Civilization? Like you didn't have time to think on the Row?"

"I mean, time away from them." Rod pointed at the sky. "I was against war and stuff that poisons our planet. The science and the technology are important, but how it's used is even more important, its capabilities. I started working with missiles and rockets. It was innocent enough. I love the universe. But then things got so dark. I saw their belief in endless warfare, their arms merchant mentality. I thought working on drones would be less damaging, then they were weaponized, too. Entities start with subtle pressure and then they put the screws to you. I think I was hypnotized to do what I did."

"Ya know what? Maybe, in a weird way, we are all hypnotized in life," Monty agreed. "Hypnotized by things like money, work, ideals, society, religion, if that's what you mean."

"Yes, that is what I mean. Modern society keeps man anesthetized with the telephone, the television, the newspaper, and the computer. All these devices take time away from people educating themselves about anything. They keep you too busy to think while you're consumed with getting your food and bills paid. Then we entertain ourselves. Distractions are designed to keep people stupid, Monty. Until you need a distraction from your distractions. Turning our minds from reason and directing it to other things, petty things. The corporate mass media keeps everyone trained on their bouncing balls."

"Well, we don't have to worry about those things anymore. Here we just have to survive and get along. Easy, right?"

"They dropped us here using parachutes, like we are butterflies burst from a cocoon, or like baby birds knocked from the nest." Rod whispered although no one nearby could hear them. "And this is no ordinary atoll. I feel better every day. Normally, we humans experience less than one percent of our reality. That is all we can perceive. Here there is more available. The introspection is a luxury."

"It's like we are civil, but it is a forced civility."

"Yeah. Buck seems ready to snap at any minute. I feel an angry undercurrent from him. How can anyone be angry in this beautiful place?" Rod said.

"Buck's a real horse's ass. He would pick a fight with a tree stump," Monty agreed.

"Buck is unenlightened. He backflashes all the time."

"Backflashes?"

"He talks back. He's contrary by nature," Rod explained. "That is backflashing. Take the high road with him."

They lapsed into quiet reflection, and then Monty spoke. "I'm trying to take the high road with Buck, but dammit there are no roads here. Sometimes I miss being alone."

"Speaking of alone, are we ever alone? Do you believe in aliens? Flight is not a modern idea. Take the Nazca lines in Peru, for instance. People don't want to accept early man was so far advanced. Like the pyramids, they are a lot older than historians admit. We still haven't figured out how the pyramids were built so accurately—perfectly lined up with the stars," Rod said. "It's arrogant to assume we are alone in the universe—look at it!" Rod made a wide sweep with his arm and began talking faster. "And there's a power right here, Monty." Rod patted the rock. "Maybe some connection we lost in the concrete jungle. Everything has energy. Do you feel it? It's a feeling something is trying to break through into awareness."

"Yeah, buddy, the power of suggestion." Monty laughed at Rod becoming spun up. "We all gotta have some mysteries, I guess." He stood up to head back to the tent. "Looking up at the universe, I just feel...small. Humbled."

"Buddy. No one's called me buddy in twenty years. You may be my first real friend since I was incarcerated. I wish we had met earlier," Rod said over his shoulder to Monty, which made Monty sad at the thought of a genius of science being without a friend for so long.

CHAPTER 18: Washington Field Office

Detailed maps of the atoll papered the office walls in the places no monitors hung. The garbage can was brimming over with take-out boxes.

After a tense weekend vacation with his wife, Agent Bledsoe arrived with his cup of afternoon coffee. Branson and Agent O'Neill had manned the boards during Bledsoe's absence.

O'Neill greeted him with a chipper, "Hello, sailor!"

"Tell me something new. Anyone talked yet?" Bledsoe inquired.

"Nope." Branson munched some Cheetos from the vending machine and swiveled in his chair.

"Nothing out of Hot Rod?"

"Well, nothing of note. The wheel is turning, but the hamster is dead. Rod's mentioned his former occupation, conspiracy theories, and the drones flying around, but it's over the others' heads, literally," O'Neill replied.

Branson licked the cheese dust from his fingers. "Oh, they dug out their microchips and threw them in the ocean," he added.

"Shit. We won't have an easy fix on their positions. Is Rod scribbling?" Bledsoe prodded Branson.

"Nope. And the cannibal's still solo, so he isn't talking to anyone."

"No one's singing 'The Fuck-Ups Greatest Hits' by the Island Gang?"

Branson snorted.

O'Neill said, "Heh. Nope. Though Lazarus—I mean Guerrero—likes to sing and Doyle likes to whistle that old chestnut from *The Bridge on the River Kwai*. It's contagious. Now Branson is whistling it too. Oh, and they tattooed themselves. Lubbuck built a sandcastle and got nipped by a shark."

Bledsoe shook his head in disappointment. "I heard the Abrahamsons are offering ten million dollars for the location of their daughter's bones. Not that we could accept it directly, but in donations or a grant. Ten million dollars." Bledsoe chewed his lip.

"The Bureau tried for years to get details from the cannibal about the bodies," Branson replied. "Frankly, I don't think there's much left of them."

O'Neill began fanning his face.

"The boys in West Virginia who remotely monitored him 24/7 said the cannibal wasn't a talker and was quite comfortable living in isolation at SCU," Branson continued. "The other inmates on the island are too busy enjoying their newfound freedom to chatter very much about the past. By all accounts, Hot Rod Cooper was always a blank. He didn't have visitors and his random chatter was always tinfoil hat stuff."

"I know that, and you know that, but Equal Op Overstreet seems to think men will act like Girl Scouts around the campfire and start yacking it up, spilling their deepest, darkest secrets. So, nothing from Davenport either?"

"Nope. He still has amnesia," Branson replied.

O'Neill said, "Did Jessica think it would be like a fireside confessional out there?" O'Neill put on a goofy voice. "'Hey, Menschen, I dropped the skull of Leah Abrahamson in the La Brea tar pits.' 'Oh really, Cannibal, well, I have information on a super weapon.' 'You don't say. Well, I was framed by the government.'"

"Maybe it's time to offer them some incentives," Bledsoe said.

"Incentives?" Branson scolded. "They are alive and in a better locale than us. This operation becoming public is a shitstorm already. We can't be seen giving them anything else. Let's wait. Don't be so impatient."

Bledsoe pushed the point. "Well, we can't be seen. Seen is the operative word. Also, we need to keep an eagle eye on the perimeter drones. We got a call from a source that an Israeli group is threatening to get as close as they can legally then dump poisoned goodies into the slipstream."

Branson shook his head. "Putting the cannibal in this group was a bad call. I don't care what the psychologists said about the theory of a boogeyman pushing their emotional buttons. Few people really know about Cooper, Doyle or Guerrero. No one really cares about them. Yeah, many heard about Lubbuck and Davenport. But of course the media was going to seize on and push the cannibal, because he's a cannibal. He garners attention, which we don't need."

"True," Bledsoe stated, "but there's no point in rearguing the situation. At least right now the public is inundated with daily media about the expanding size of the Kardashians' derrieres and Bruce's life after his sex change. They'll move on to the upcoming election and the Donald Trump circus. They are and will be thoroughly distracted."

"I think it was really brave of Caitlyn," O'Neill offered. "It's all a sideshow, really."

What started as Project Island X was approved into operational status in 2014. Judging by the composition of the group of resulting inmates, you wouldn't think the government spent much time choosing the men and human interplay involved. You'd be wrong. A small, compartmentalized team consisting of a sociologist, two psychologists, a doctor, and a hypnotist were consulted on strategies and techniques. They selected these prisoners for a reason.

CHAPTER 19: Mis'ries of Island Life

Since they were missing all synthetic amenities, bitching among the men about deprivation was evitable until they adapted. The island offered no comfort or security, and very little in the way of material possessions. Every day they discovered more about their new home, and not all of it was good. For instance, the land was pervaded by insects and swarming with non-native black rats. Food had to be eaten and stored away carefully or it would be immediately set upon by marauders. Monty's patience began ebbing like the tide once his supplies were attacked in his tent. He gazed discouragingly at his remaining MRE with a freshly gnawed corner.

"Damn. My sack got raided. The rats had a feast. They laid siege to my MREs. I have one half-chewed MRE left now. Dammit to hell and back! Will hanging stuff up keep them off our food?"

"That's what happens when you sit on MREs," Buck snorted with derision.

Even before their MREs started to run low, food discussions became the number one obsession. Had they not come from prison, they would have complained even more about the lack of variety in their diet. They had agreed not to talk about taboo subjects like their personal MREs and view them like they had their prison canteen items. But Buck didn't give a shit. Unmindful of the others' yearning, or perhaps because of it, he enjoyed eating his supplies out in the open and chewing with his mouth ajar, observing their reactions. Even tipping a coconut up to his lips, his eyes always watched the others. After he consumed the MRE's contents, he'd turn the bag inside out and suck on it.

"Wait. Did you find any seeds or grains in your MREs?" Trent asked. "Because when I open mine, I'm sifting through them."

Buck sniggered. "In meats and pastas?"

"Oh. Maybe we got different varieties. If someone finds a grain or a seed, it can be planted. So be on the lookout," Trent continued.

Lazarus smacked his lips while reposing in the afternoon heat. "Last night I dreamed of fried chicken. I'm dying for some chicken. Let's catch a bird and roast it in coconut milk."

Rod was dismantling some Diet Coke cans he'd collected on salvage hunts, carefully removing the tops. "Those red-footed boobies are the cutest birds I've ever seen. I couldn't eat those. No. No. They are so inquisitive that some of them will come right up to me. They haven't developed a fear of people."

"You have a weird chemistry with creatures, don't you?" Monty remarked, thinking of bird flesh.

Rod blushed. "I guess I pick up on things other people don't. It's an intuitive sense."

Buck let out an exaggerated burp. "Roast me a big ole booby. I'm almost tapped out of supplies. And I've got a headache."

"Me too. My mouth has been dry for days. Is my tongue turning white?" Rod stuck out his tongue toward Monty. "I've had a really dry mouth."

"Y'all are probably dehydrated by the sun," Trent said. "We need a shade structure for when we're just chillin'. A big one so that we can keep a fire lit underneath it."

"Good idea, son," Lazarus said.

Within a short span of two weeks, everyone's enthusiasm seemed slightly dampened by the heat. Every pore on their bodies was open and sweating.

"It's brutal, this humidity. It's like a damn sweat lodge without a pipe. I'm dying out here. This is not the same sun as anywhere else in the world." Buck moved in a stank-legged motion to shift his soaked shorts stuck to his crotch.

Trent constantly scratched the bites covering his body, many of which were bleeding and oozing because he would not leave them alone. "These bugs are driving me crazy. I can't stand it. Back when I smoked and tweaked I used to think there were bugs in my skin. I'd pick at them with needles, tweezers, X-ACTO knives. But this is worse. Now they are actually real and on me. And I'm out of spray. They are banging me everywhere. No place is sacred, not even my eyelids." Trent tried to scratch his back with a stick.

"Do me a favor, man," Trent asked Lazarus.

"What?"

"Scratch my back. There's a spot I can't reach."

Lazarus obliged him.

"I still got spray," Buck announced proudly.

Trent looked at Buck. "I'll trade you an MRE for the rest of your spray."

Jumping into their discussion, Lazarus instructed Trent sternly. "You don't need to do that, son. Also, your hands are dirty when you're scratching. Quit scratching or infection will set in."

"What if you go and sit in the lagoon up to your neck? That'll give you some relief." Monty added, agreeing with Lazarus. He didn't like Buck angling for anyone else's MREs.

"And have a shark tear a leg off? No, thanks. Why do these insects like me so much? They are barely touching Laz," Trent lamented.

"My hide's too tough," Lazarus replied, untroubled by the fiendish mosquitoes. He stopped scratching Trent. "I'm tired of hearing whiny shit. We're all getting attacked. You can't stay in the tent to avoid them. Let Rod spot for you and sit in the lagoon. The salt will heal you up."

"Four MREs for the rest of my bug spray," Buck offered. "Relief in a bottle. Whaddya say? Whaddya say?"

Lazarus laughed as if Buck's offer was beyond the pale. "You loco. What make you think he got four left?"

Monty stopped himself from joining in further.

"Two MREs," Trent counteroffered.

"You acting fucking stupid." Lazarus shook his head at Trent. "Come to terms with it. Use your willpower."

"He's a big boy. He can make his own deal," Buck pushed, not making eye contact with Lazarus. "Three MREs and the spray is yours. Come on. I only used it on the first day."

Trent caved, striking a bargain with Buck. He gave Buck two MREs for a ¾ full bottle of insect repellent. Trent liberally doused his sunburned and bitten skin with a layer of bug spray. He held the bottle up to the sun. "Are you sure you didn't water this down?

Buck hooted and shook his head.

Trent frowned sullenly. "It's runny."

CHAPTER 20: The Kidnapper – Shane "Buck" Lubbuck

Shane Lubbuck had a poor start in life. His abusive childhood became apparent when he was found by social services bruised, hungry and wet in his crib. His mother did not hold him enough in infancy. A few years later it was discovered he suffered from hearing loss in one ear, likely due to a beating. Even though he was eventually adopted into a new home, he still felt unwanted and like a nobody.

He started stealing Matchbox cars in elementary school, then graduated to petty theft of cigarettes and beer by middle school. He set fire to a neighbor's shed because he was jealous of their son's three-wheeler inside, sparking a visit to juvenile hall. He nicked anything that was not nailed down. Buck wasn't picky; he stole from everyone, even his adopted family, when he wasn't spending a goodly amount of time in juvie being arrogant and asocial. He chalked his acting out up to having a low tolerance for stupidity. He was the kind of guy who relished burning his bridges with an acetylene torch. When he was sent to jail, he decried it as "summer camp for fuckups."

As an adult, Buck was emotionally impotent in his relationships. When Buck kept a job, he did manual labor. Sometimes he stole from clients, nothing they would ever expect someone to steal. One day he was laying marble floor in an upscale Ohio neighborhood. The client was a wealthy land developer who made some wisecrack about Buck's ponytail. The comment rankled Buck terribly, stirring up everything in him that felt inferior. The owner represented to Buck the sort of person he hated the most. After feeling looked down upon over the offhand comments, miniscule wages, and the multiple times he had to redo certain areas to satisfy the owner, Buck decided to abduct their daughter for ransom.

He stewed on his plan for six weeks, including a month after the job's completion. When his day was going particularly poorly, he kept remembering the insults: "Are you stupid or something?" "Can't you hear me, or is your ponytail in the way?" and "What is this? Hippies laying tile?" In his private snooping, Buck had found a folder for an offshore bank account that currently held a small balance, complete with passwords. He stole the paperwork. He considered having the father transfer the ransom money to the offshore account, and not even mess with trying a drop. With his impulsive mind made up, he went to their residence in the wee hours, opened the unlocked basement window, and snuck inside. The house was so large they didn't hear a sound. The stepmother, having consumed her nightly dose of sleeping pills, was out to the world. It was essentially a stranger abduction. Surprisingly for Buck, being a lifelong thief, he did little rifling of their property. Instead, he focused on the family's greatest treasure, Melissa. He slapped duct tape on the little girl's mouth, tied her up with her pink shoelaces, shoved her inside a sports duffel bag, the kind with breathable holes, left out a back door and put her in his car trunk. Wrestling her into the bag was both clumsy and stupid. For an alibi, he went to his next tile job in the early morning.

Melissa was found missing from her bed by her stepmother. Because she belonged to a wealthy family who courted the media, adorable pictures of the child aired on television at every commercial break. *Distraught Parents Plea "Free Our Honey Bee"* tugged at the heartstrings of the close-knit community and spread throughout the nation. The federal kidnapping statute allowed the authorities to get involved immediately. The activated AMBER Alert Plan blasted urgent bulletins in the child abduction case to everyone's telephones. The Emergency Alert System aired pictures and the description of the missing child and her assumed abductor. Problem was, the information on the abductor was inaccurate. Because of an ongoing custody battle, the police surmised the child's natural mother had absconded with her. Regardless, the police searched her neighborhood door-to-door. Many in the sleepy community of Chagrin Falls embarked in an extensive and frantic effort to find her by passing out flyers, scouring rural areas, and holding candlelight vigils. Officers and volunteers scoured day and night, calling out her name, using flashlights and searchlights crisscrossing each other in the shadows, searching. Her disappearance shook the community to its core.

Unbeknownst to the anxious volunteers, their efforts were in vain.

Buck's plan to ransom the little girl was foiled when she died inside the duffel from the heat and her chronic asthma. Once he found she was in early-stage rigor mortis, he zipped the case shut and cursed. Buck, pissed off about the foiling of his plan, couldn't be bothered with returning her body. Freaking out, he dumped her, taking no lengths at concealment. He tossed the bag off a bridge like a sack of potatoes into the water. The river eagerly swallowed up the heavy duffel. Little did Buck realize, an old luggage tag from his last trip to New York remained balled up inside the duffel's pocket. Had she not started stiffening, he would have searched it. The duffel eventually surfaced five days later and was spotted floating on the top of the river by two boys. They waded out and used a branch to snag it, hoping it contained pirate treasure. What they saw scarred them for life. The location where the bag was found became a makeshift memorial site with mourners blanketing the shoreline with candles and teddy bears.

Once arrested and named, the public bayed for Buck's blood. Nothing solidifies a small community as when evil visits its doors. Local TV news stations carried the child's funeral live. Due to heavy publicity, Buck's trial was moved to a town 72 miles away. His bad attitude did not help his case. His public defender argued that at worst Buck was guilty of only abduction/kidnapping and second-degree murder because she died of an asthma attack. The prosecution argued for both first-degree murder and kidnapping. Unable or unwilling to heed his attorney's advice, during sentencing Buck stood up to make a blame-shifting statement insulting the victim's father. "I ain't gonna lie, but she told me she didn't want to go back home. She said her dad was mean and touched her private parts."

During his prison stint at Terre Haute, Buck's behavioral problems continued. He particularly enjoyed verbally provoking the staff and throwing his feces at the guards. He attempted to escape. Federal law allows prisoners to practice any religion without any outward commitments to prove their faith, so he constantly changed his religious affiliation simply for food, perks, and convenience. If there was an advantage to take, Buck took it. His inclusion on Island X was an extension of this concept.

CHAPTER 21: What's for Dinner?

Monty awoke to a low-grade headache, which he was loath to medicate with his small stash of Advil. The sounds of the night's shrilling crickets and the monotonous hum of mosquitoes turned into an incessant tinnitus-like ringing in his ears, like they'd flown inside his head and got stuck there.

Lazarus woke up declaring it was the day to catch a bird. "I am going hunting. What's everyone doing?"

"We are low on wood and we need old husks, too," Trent remarked. "It'll be easier if we divide up tasks. Every day we'll need food and general supplies like crab, eggs, and firewood. And I know it's wasteful, but having two fires will make it less likely they will both burn out when it rains. One fire can go under a teepee-like structure."

"Good idea, son," Lazarus said.

"I'd like to give fishing a try," Monty said. "Hunting's not my bailiwick."

Buck couldn't resist commenting. "Bailiwick? Who says that? Some old fucker in a powdered wig?" Buck imitated Monty to perfection.

Monty felt his feathers ruffled like a bird standing the wrong way in the wind.

"I'll gather then," Trent said. "Cooking is not my strong suit. Being burned once is enough. I really don't wanna deal with fire every day. I'm tired of making sure it doesn't burn out."

"That's okay. Your job is to use your whistling to ward off Somali pirates," Buck snarked.

Monty would have laughed if he didn't detest Buck.

When they looked at Buck to see what task he'd voluntarily take on, he pointed a deflecting finger at Rod in the distance, who was whittling a spear with a rock. Rod's energy came in bursts and then he tended to lapse into long silences. Rod, in the middle of an energy spurt, was on his second spear.

"What's his strength?" Buck gestured to Rod. Unlike the others, little heed was paid to Rod.

"Isn't it obvious?" Monty replied.

Buck smiled dismissively. "Enlighten me."

"Trainspotting and weaponry," Monty said in slow, measured tones. "With his keen eye for happenings and telling you about them, he would have saved your ass from that shark had you listened to him. Someone has to watch out as we rest or go about our business. He's perfect for that. Have you seen that spear he made for Lazarus?"

"Well, good for him. I don't need a job. We are free from rules now," Buck said. "Life here should be uncomplicated."

"True. But there are still consequences in life, natural consequences. Even the insects have an organized society. The ants have tasks. The bees have jobs," Monty remarked.

While weighing his new spear in hand, Lazarus declared, "You wanna eat something other than crab and eggs? You gonna have to get off your ass. Time to stick your oar in the water. There's no charity cases here. Sack up or pack up!"

"Say please." Buck sniggered, then thought better of verbally poking at Lazarus while he held a weapon. Buck capitulated, sighing loudly. "Fine then. I'll fish, too. I got a debt to settle anyway. I'm gonna regain my self-respect by stabbing me a motherfuckin' shark. Payback. Lemme see that spear you're working on, Hot Rod." When Buck held Rod's crafted and perfectly weighted spear, he said, "You may not be totally useless after all. Tell me all your secrets, Hot Rod."

"Leave him alone," Lazarus said.

Monty advised Buck not to try for a shark that was too large. "You'll just poke it and lose the spear when it darts off."

"I know what I'm doing, old man. I don't need lessons from you. Or maybe you are practiced at poking stuff? Now, what is best to use as bait?"

"Get the StarKist tuna logo tattooed on your shoulder and they come," Lazarus deadpanned.

On the trip to the lagoon, Buck's talk annoyed Monty to no end. "So did the feds really say they may send more inmates here? Or was that something you cooked up?"

"It's what an agent told me," Monty replied.

"Which one?"

"Agent John Bledsoe."

Buck barked. "Yeah, Bledsoe. I met him. That dude is full of himself. What a choad. The name Bledsoe makes me think, 'Well, your Honor, I hit him so hard he bled so much.'"

Monty didn't laugh at Buck's comment.

"They didn't tell me nothing about this place," Buck continued. "So, do you think they will dump a ton of convicts here and squeeze us together like some death row Auschwitz?"

"Their intentions are unknown to me," Monty replied stiffly.

"Hey, would your family be able to rescue you off this island?"

"If they were able to pull strings I wouldn't have been on death row in the first place," Monty responded.

"Maybe they'll surprise you with an escape. Who would you take with you? You must hate being around us criminals, with you being all innocent."

"I like it here so far," Monty replied.

"You're getting close to Hot Rod. Did he tell you about his theories? You think he's crazy?"

"No," Monty said. "He's eccentric."

When they arrived at the lagoon, Buck said, "The way the fog forms here is not normal."

Using a mosquito net as a dragnet, Monty tried to capture some fish at the lagoon's shoreline. But he wasn't Jesus and the fish didn't jump into his trap. Monty watched as Buck attempted his payback. Buck began by tossing raw crab guts as chum into the water, then lobbing and thrusting around at any guests. At first Buck seemed to take perverse glee in it, but after an hour the effort wore thin. Struggling with impatience, flinging about invectives, he finally broke the spear in half in a rage when he failed to catch anything. "Screw this place! These sharks are a fucking menace!" Buck seethed.

Monty couldn't hold back. "Just so you know, Rod spent an entire night making that spear."

Buck spun around and gritted his teeth, still holding the sharp broken tip in one hand. "Use the stick up your ass and catch some yourself. Why are you always riding me, huh?" Buck attempted to gain control. "You're good, you know that? Putting ideas in everyone's minds. You use your advice to feel superior. Do you need to control everyone, or just me?"

Monty fingered the sharpened spork in his pants. *This guy could kill me, right here, right now. Shove me into the lagoon and let the sharks take the evidence.* Monty chose non-reaction and backed away. "Sorry. I was only telling you he put effort into that spear. This fishing is going nowhere. I'm heading back." Monty left first, forcing himself not to look back, while imagining what Buck could do to him with that tip.

"What's for dinner?" Trent asked upon Buck's empty-handed return.

"The shark I stabbed got away," Buck lied, rubbing his sunburned left ear.

Monty blew out the side of his mouth.

"I'm making a large pen, a coop for the crabs, with a palm frond top. As we scare them up we can chuck them in for our feasts. That's easy enough," Trent said.

"You're appointed sergeant of the coop," Buck said.

Before sundown Lazarus brought back two birds, terns so as not to upset Rod, declaring, "Island boobies don't got much meat on 'em." He threw one tern at Trent and the other at Buck. "Start plucking. Pull off the feathers and save 'em for a pillow. One day we'll all have down bedding."

"We can make rope beds and line them with feather quilts," Trent said.

"Whatever. Get plucking," Lazarus commanded.

That night the island slept. But Monty could not relax. He felt an expectancy, like he was waiting for something to happen. The dynamic with Buck did not help Monty's mental state. That evening he had a prophetic dream, a night terror. He confided to Rod at watch. "I dreamed I was paralyzed. Someone was killing my wife and she was calling my name. I couldn't move. I was riveted by our ceiling fan going around and around in circles. I don't know it if was a memory or what. Some of my memories are magnified. Others are erased."

"Mmm, you had a psychic break. Wait. You were paralyzed but could hear the others?"

"Yes. I could feel the ceiling fan blowing on my face and hear the gurgling and odd whispering. And the smell of defecation. Maybe I dreamed of it because Buck said I was a master at poking things."

"Your family was politically connected. Maybe someone else did it. Maybe it was a conspiracy. Political candidates are like legs of the same octopus. Maybe your family quit playing ball with them. The government charged *me* with conspiracy and that is ironic because they are the true conspirators. They are think tanks that try to manipulate how and what people think. If anything will wake you up, this island will."

CHAPTER 22: Tension

Monty, Rod, Trent, and Lazarus took advantage of the daily rain showers to bathe, and greatly concerned themselves with hanging up and tucking away their towels when done. Due to the humidity nothing stayed completely dry. Lazarus was fastidious with his grooming, or what was left to be groomed.

However, as the days progressed the men were looking seedier, wilder, and unkempt. Like the island, they took on a weather-beaten aspect. Their beards and toenails grew quickly. Their hair became stringy or matted. Their skin became mottled with sunspots. Their sedentary lifestyle was but a memory as they regressed to the primitive. Their hands became calloused. They sported scratches on their arms and faces. And tensions accumulated like the dirt under their broken fingernails.

"Dude, you stink!"

"I smell like yesterday. We all smell alike now."

Failing to catch any fish the previous day, Buck pretended to tidy up the camp. By afternoon he was slouching around like he was missing vertebrae, turning the pages of his survival book. But Monty noted Buck's mouth was slack-jawed, and his empty eyes were really staring out to sea.

Like the constant friction that creates smoke that bursts into fire, the smoke began when the newly crafted spear Buck carelessly left on the shore floated out on a wave. Trent had to swim out to retrieve it after Rod squealed.

"Anytime you want to help," Trent muttered under his breath to Buck. That was the start of a bad scene.

Monty unknowingly continued the tension when he criticized the crab Buck cooked. Spitting out a mouthful, he said, "This is infused with stink. It smells rotten."

Buck bristled and deflected in return. "Hoity-toity! We don't all have your high standards. Are we rubbing elbows with the Queen? Not all of us were born with a silver spoon in our mouth."

Lazarus bent down and sniffed the preparation rock next to the fire, the one on which Buck left both shells and a warm gut pile. "The prep rock is dirtier than the inside of a piggy bank. And it reeks. Abombao! You have to scrub it off after using it. Don't go leaving anything raw like guts or shit laying on it. Quit pussy-footing around, jacking off, and do something around here."

"Money has nothing to do with cleanliness," Trent piled on. "I sold junk at the scrapyard and I used to raid the rusty change out of water fountains for food. And even I know to clean off our only cooking plate. This isn't skid row." Trent had taken to sitting in the smoke's fire to avoid insects.

"Wait. Skid Row? I love that band. 'Eighteen and life.'" Lazarus belted out lyrics and pretended to whip his non-existent hair around like the lead singer.

"Whatever, you guys. Just grab another rock." Buck flung out his arm in anger. "Want to rake me over the coals?" He pointed at Monty. "And you, quit using Lazarus as your mouthpiece. How did you manage to fuck up, Trust Fund?" Buck counted off on his fingers. "No poverty. No abuse. No neglect. No crazy family. Unlike the rest of us, you had to try pretty hard to fuck up." Buck's words dripped with hostility.

Monty stopped stoking the fire and shot back through gritted teeth. "Listen to the bigmouth. Why do you always reduce me to dollar signs? 'Cause you care about money! You're pretty high-minded for someone who snatched a little girl out of her bed for ransom. Tied her up and duct taped her mouth, wasn't it, and threw her in a suitcase in the trunk of your car to cook her brain. All for a little money."

"You did what?" Lazarus raised his eyebrows in alarm. "Hold up. What? A little girl? You said it was a chica."

Outraged, with his hands on his hips, Buck bowed up on Monty. "Well you poked a thousand holes in three people while they were drugged out. You claim you don't remember anything. I learned from all my shit and copped to it. It built my character."

"Well then, I suppose you have a lot of character," Monty responded icily. "Tell them it isn't true. Tell them you didn't abduct a little girl for money...and let her die."

"They ain't interested in history, or so they said. So shut your blow hole!" Buck snarled and lunged at Monty. His hands slapped Monty's chest, pushing him backward.

"Oh no! Oh n-no!" Rod gasped in alarm and shrank away from the group. "Stop! Stop!"

Jumping between them as nimbly as a boxer, Lazarus shoved Buck into the sand. Ferocity flashed across his face like a burst of summer lightning. "Step to me and my homies and you are on your own. This is your only warning. Who you gonna turn to then?"

Buck grasped for an ally. "Why do you always take his side? I'm the only one here who only harmed one person, and it was a fucking accident." Buck raised a single digit in defiance. "If we play 'who is the biggest scumbag,' it ain't me! I took responsibility for what I did. Did he? 'Fugue state,' my sore ass. You believe the murders just slipped his fucking mind? Poking holes in people just slipped his mind? He's the type of person whose money bought him everything!"

"Death row leveled us all, did it not?" Monty yelled back. "The lofty and the lowly alike, so shut up."

Lazarus spat on the sand, purposely missing Buck by an inch but pressing the threat. "Take a walk. Last warning, pendejo."

Buck stood up, eyed them hard, and began strolling away slowly, as if the others did not threaten him in the slightest.

"Thank you. Thank you," Rod mumbled in distress at Buck's back.

Later that night, Monty spoke to Rod in frustration. "I can't sleep. I haven't slept well in years. When I used to ask the doctors at SCU for some meds to help I was told sleep is optional."

"It's no surprise. The moon is full." Rod pointed at the round moon with its mirror image gleaming off the water. "Today has all the telltale signs of full-moon madness. Every civilization of man has been interested in the moon. Even the Magi in your Bible, the Three Wise Men, were supposedly astronomers. Ninety percent of a human being is composed of water. And the moon pulls on water. Scientists say it doesn't affect us, but who knows, maybe it does," Rod surmised.

"Or maybe the tension is not the moon but on account of Buck being an asshole."

Rod laughed. "Or it could be that."

"Why is there still violence here?" Monty said. "Why can't we get over ourselves?"

"You could walk for a hundred years looking for a place with no sorrow, pain, or violence. You'd never find it. This place is born of violence, if you think about it. A volcano is a violent explosion. Even ants kill by strategic attack. Humans should try to overcome it, transcend it. Recognize and learn to live with the elemental forces. Look at things with the eye of the mind. I think we need to consider not only about the dynamics of our group but also the good of mankind and for the plants, animals, and the earth. I fight against my fear all the time. Fear keeps us from seeing anything accurately."

"I'll tell you, fear can make people crazy. Remember Salem?" Monty offered.

"They were caught in a terror spiral. Crazy. People called me crazy for years and said I should die for it. But what is worse? Hurting someone when you're not right in the head, or being right in the head and still hurting someone? You said you couldn't remember the murders you were convicted of. In Scientology, you'd never have gotten away with not remembering your incident. Auditing would find some memories for you." Rod laughed bitterly. "I guess you'll remember when you are ready to remember, Monty. Then you'll sleep."

Monty walked back to the tent and closed the flap against the mosquitoes. He didn't know if he really wanted to remember the past.

Still perched on the lookout rock, Rod used his peripheral vision and sense of smell. "I can see you, you know," Rod said into the night.

The outline of a man took a step forward. His eyes were shining silver in the dark.

"What do you need? We're not bothering you. Go away because they've marked you. Stay away."

The shadow loomed for a minute just outside the light of the moon and then slowly retreated.

CHAPTER 23: Fate

The next morning a peculiar pall hung over the men. Monty accompanied Lazarus on his hunt. "Not even two weeks in and we're already fighting. Should I be worried about Buck?" Monty asked.

"If it goes sideways I got your back against that kiddie killer. I got Trent's back. I even got Hot Rod's back, as scared of his shadow as he is."

"Buck's aimless and lazy; he's a half-measure. That's his real problem. He's smart but he's a sloth. He does the smallest amount of work humanly possible to get by," Monty noted. "And he's constantly jerking my chain. Do you think kidnapping that little girl was the only serious crime he ever committed?"

"No. You wearing a shank like I told you?"

"Yes." Monty nodded and continued complaining. "Manipulation is the pattern of Buck's life. Like exploiting those gullible women from prison, or working Trent out of those MREs with watered-down bug spray. And I didn't tell you before, but he threatened me out at the lagoon that day he went hunting for shark. My tolerance for him is capped out. He's an impenetrable asshole. And frankly, I'm becoming ambivalent about his well-being."

"Don't let him see you bothered. He keep goin' then," Lazarus said. "He gets your goat, names it, and eats it."

"I try not to let him get to me. Sometimes I think this island is more hostile than us. We're in the Pacific, a word which implies calm, but that's not accurate. Not accurate at all. There's something off about her, like a Garden of Eden. She's pretty to look at, a dream, an artifice, like a postcard or a picture, with a veneer of hospitality, but she's evil and filled with pestilence."

"You mean she pretty but she got disease and vermin?" Lazarus hooted. "Yo, she got crabs too."

"And we eat her crabs," Monty added with a wry sideways smile. "So what does that say about us? That we're her parasites? I won't deny the universe has a sense of humor. This place feels like a final destination. These palms remind me of *Hotel California*. Remember that album cover?"

"Who doesn't?" Lazarus launched into the guitar solo.

"You know that song's about drugs, right?" Monty asked, trying to interrupt him.

"Nah, it's about a chica."

Before Lazarus completed the wailing guitar finale a loud dashing and smashing in the brush ahead startled them. Lazarus placed his fingers to his lips. Lazarus went left and Monty to the right. Monty exhausted himself in hot pursuit of phantom sounds. He made his way back to camp.

CHAPTER 24: Hansi's Duffel Bag

Monty was splashing salt water on his face when Lazarus came running back to camp. Between ragged breaths, Lazarus told the others what Monty had already said.

"I swear we heard something big running through the bushes. It's him unless there's a bear or a moose here. I chased it through the jungle. We need to go and find out what the motherfucker is up to." Lazarus, bathed in paranoia, exhorted, "What if he tries to pillage our village?"

Tuning in to Lazarus's panic, Trent said, "We don't want him to take us unaware."

"I haven't seen hide nor hair of him," Buck said. "Someone would have crossed paths with him. It was probably some animal. You heard a rat, or your Chewbacca thing."

"Chupacabra," Lazarus corrected him. "Listen, I believe in da chupa because my abuela, my grandmother, found one dead on her farm in Puerto Rico. She said it was stinky, gray and hairless with long teeth. But the vultures picked it clean and tore it up before police came."

"I doubt the cannibal is alive," Buck said. "We haven't heard him tramping around. He can't have a fire 'cause we would have smelled it or seen the smoke, unless he's way on the other side of the island.

He should be out of MREs unless he's supplementing."

Rod said, "He could be eating them cold or maybe he ate some poisoned fish."

"Well, if he's dead there's no harm in taking his supplies," Monty said. "Rod, could you stay here and mind the camp? Do what you do best."

The four men set out to ambush the cannibal. After walking the circuit of the island's shoreline and finding no clues, they went in deeper.

"Look out for booby traps and snares. Who knows what's enveloped in all this vegetation," Trent warned as they picked their way carefully through the jungle. The air hung thick with humidity and they picked up mosquitoes as they ventured along.

"Where this scumbag?" Lazarus muttered.

"Well, there is always that one area of town," Monty said sarcastically.

The gang searched as stealthily as they could manage. With Trent tracking, they stumbled across Hans's camp on the other side of the island, more than twenty minutes' walk in one of the densest sections of the jungle almost choked out by twisting vines, foliage, and overgrown greenery. Located like a tree house, four feet off the ground, it was so camouflaged as to be barely discernable. They narrowly avoided the viny thorns craftily woven like barbed wire snares. Hans was nowhere in sight.

Lazarus pointed a direction for everyone to go. They moved fast.

"Whoa. Look at this setup." Monty climbed in and emitted a low whistle through his teeth at the carefully executed structure with the tightly set hewn limbs. "German efficiency."

"Mira mira. These branches, they've been sawn." Lazarus ran his fingers over the outside. "This is loco. Why did they give him tools?"

Monty rubbed the even edge of a large branch. "I agree. These were cut by a sharp instrument. He couldn't have made a tool this advanced, could he?"

Searching around, the group became more agitated. Trent located Hans's burned-out fire pit at the back of his structure.

"Oh my god. He's got a cooking pot." Trent pointed to a metal object suspended on a rod by two Y-sticks. "And what's this? A bone pile?"

Monty found and threw down Hans's backpack and the duffel bag. Immediately, Buck started rummaging through them. "And a hand shovel. He's had who-knows-what kind of tools this whole damn time." Buck curled his lip in anger. "I want to know how he came about this."

"Maybe he didn't build this camp. Maybe the government already had this built when they scouted the island and the cannibal found it?" Trent said.

"The feds overlooking a detail? Say it ain't so!" Buck snickered.

"What the hell? What the fuck is this?" Trent, who joined in pawing through Hans's backpack, brandished a book.

"That's the Torah. It's a Jewish Bible," Monty said after glancing down at it. Trent looked perplexed so Monty explained further. "Kind of like the Old Testament, the five books of Moses. You know, before Jesus."

"Why's he got this?" Lazarus grabbed the Torah from Trent and waved it around. "This is for some black witchcraft blasphemy. He killed and ate Jews. Is he wiping his culo with the pages? Why did they give him this? This is bullshit."

Monty said, "I'll take the Torah."

"Didn't he convert in prison?" Buck asked.

Lazarus ignored Buck when he saw the MREs. "Matzo and grape juice. Fucking macaroons!" Lazarus flicked through the pile, seizing on the packages, and elbowing over them protectively.

"No way. No way. I love macaroons," Trent cried out, his eyes rolling in ecstasy.

Buck licked his chapped lips. "I betcha this stuff is kosher. Special dietary shit. He probably requested it. Wish I had thought of that."

With their heads almost together, they rifled through the freeze-dried meals. Monty tossed down Hans's blue tarp and gray blanket. "Let's go."

Without consulting anyone Lazarus made the unilateral decision. "We are confiscating this. Fucking macaroons! We're taking all his supplies as punishment. Leave him to the elements." He begun stuffing everything back into the duffel—the MREs, the small shovel, and the supplies—muttering, "This is some bullshit. He had a pot and tools and didn't share them? We've been busting our hands and cutting ourselves. Grab the tarp, son."

Trent slung Hans's blue tarp and blanket over his shoulder and snatched the pot.

Back aground again, Monty marveled at the lair and the pride in its craftsmanship. "The cannibal must have a machete somewhere. These are clean edges. Look at them. And what are these weird markings?" Strange angular symbols were etched and scratched into the bark and surrounding rock.

"Come on, let's hustle. Leave him a message, Monty," Lazarus said.

Monty used a stick to sign a terse scrawl, in a nervous hand, into the dirt that read: *Come to drop site.* No one said anything when Buck left another sign by pissing on the entry like a dog marking his territory.

On the way back to camp they jabbered excitedly. Trent asked, "What if he arms himself?

What if he made poison darts or something? Those Germans love poison."

"Lace up," Lazarus commanded. "Everyone get your shanks and strip down. Don't leave him a handhold."

"The cannibal may not even need a weapon. Who here has killed multiple people with his bare hands? Because he has. Experience counts," Buck warned. "He looks like a neck snapper."

Rod paled visibly when he saw the men walking back to camp with Hans's appropriated blue tarp and supplies. Rod held an unwarlike sock filled with rocks, which was the furthest he was willing to go to make a weapon. Interrupting and talking over one another, they quickly filled him in on their find. When Lazarus told Rod to arm himself with a sharp object Rod scrunched up his face. "Wait. Isn't that what they want us to do? Kill him, I mean. They are watching us and expecting us to attack each other. We are playing right into their hands. Isn't there a compromise?" His nose imitated a fearful rabbit's movement.

"Compromise?" Lazarus argued. "Compromise makes you weak. If he picks us off one by one at night we become weak, you know what I mean?"

"But it's morally wrong," Rod insisted, risking ridicule.

"It's self-defense," Trent persuaded.

"Jungle law. No crime. No God. No jury. Morals be damned," Buck said.

"Screw it," Lazarus declared. "Let's eat those macaroons. If I die, I die with macaroon in my belly."

CHAPTER 25: Confrontation

"...we are challenging nature itself...Nature here is vile and base. I see fornication, asphyxiation, choking, fighting for survival, and growing and just rotting away. Of course, there's a lot of misery. The trees are in misery. The birds are in misery. I don't think they sing; they just screech in pain. Taking a close look at what's around us, there is some sort of harmony. There is the harmony of overwhelming and collective murder."

Werner Herzog – My Best Fiend

The cannibal came to confront them about stealing his goods. Rod, as trainspotter, saw the cannibal first. "Oh. Here he is. He's advancing! But he looks unarmed."

Hans's face and arms were sunburned lobster red and his hair was gilded golden by the sun. Other than that, he looked no worse for wear.

"It's gonna jump off," Lazarus muttered walking toward Hans, flexing his fingers for combat. A razor-sharp shiv made from a broken bottle with a melted plastic handle peeked from the back of his shorts.

Rod snatched up the thin sheet of metal he'd managed to fashion from the Coke cans. He flipped it to the shiny side, angled it upward to the sun and aimed the reflected light directly into the cannibal's eyes. "Halt!" Rod squealed.

Sunblind and shielding his eyes from a distance of about fifteen feet, Hans stopped and addressed his adversaries in monotone. "Where's my stuff? You stole my stuff."

Ignoring his comment, Lazarus puffed up like a cockatoo. "Your stuff? How did you get those tools?"

"In a bag on the beach." Hans remained stone-faced and unmoving.

"When?" Lazarus challenged.

"First day."

"You've had tools meant for all of us. We've been out here bustin' our asses, spilling blood, getting splinters in our fingers, eating off a dirty rock. Where's the machete?" Lazarus danced around, hustling from foot to foot, clasping and unclasping his hands.

Monty felt faint and spacey. He marveled at Lazarus explaining to the cannibal how they'd all been hard done by him absconding with the tools.

"No machete," Hans said.

"Don't lie to me. We saw your setup. We saw those sharp cuts on the palms."

"Bag only had a pot, shovel and a saw," he replied robotically.

"Hand over the saw."

"Buried it. Kill me and you'll never find it," Hans replied cunningly. "I know how to hide things."

"Bet you do, you Jew-hatin' chomo mofo." The insult came out like a song. Lazarus shook his head from side-to-side, biting his lower lip.

This statement finally provoked an emotional response from Hans. He winced as if slapped, balled his fists, and his face reddened further through his sunburn. "I do not hate Juden."

"We aren't giving you nothing back. Let's go. You and me. One-on-one. Then I let my homies finish you off."

"You? You're afraid of rat. And he can't fish." Hans scoffed, pointing at Lazarus then Buck, and actually smiled at his quip. As stalking was his specialty, Hans had been meticulously prowling, snooping and spying on their camp undetected.

The fight didn't go according to plan. Monty wished he could say the men went head-to-head like two powerful old bears but the battle was quick. The humiliating statement about his fear of rats was all Lazarus needed to hear. The words landed hard. Lazarus propelled himself straight for the cannibal. His head hit Hans's stomach, pushing an "oof" out of him. Quick to disarm his prey, Hans tried to grasp Lazarus's neck, but Lazarus proved to be too thick-necked and sweat-slimed to hold. As Hans's mouth went down, clamping around and engulfing Lazarus's ear, Lazarus's hand went up and found the left side of Hans's throat, driving the shank into his carotid artery. Blood came pouring out.

Hans toppled onto his side, blinking dumbly. He grasped for the weapon. A pink saliva bubble, Lazarus's blood mixed with his own, appeared around his mouth. He said, "Schicksal," and it popped.

Buck moved in and kicked Hans. "I ain't afraid of nothin'. I'm gonna use my good foot to kick your ass."

"Holy shit. Holy shit!" was all Monty could blurt out while limply holding the shank at his side. Having committed himself to this insanity, he found he was uselessly rooted to the spot. Hans was the first person he'd seen dying.

"What's he saying?" Pumped on adrenaline and bleeding freely from his ear, Lazarus, now joined by Trent and Buck, circled around Hans. "What chomo saying?"

"Shick-saw?" Trent ventured.

Monty shook off his paralysis. "I don't know. I don't speak German, but shiksa is the Yiddish word for a girl—a gentile, a non-Jewish girl." Monty stared at the shiv lodged in the cannibal's neck, thinking of that horrible ice pick in Angela's neck. *I didn't do it.*

"You ain't getting no shiksas in Hell, chomo." Mimicking Buck, Lazarus kicked Hans in the ribs with his bare feet. "Where's that saw?"

"Das ist mein…Schicksal," were his last groaning words. *This is my destiny.* Hans's eyes rolled upward, staring at the sun.

Breathing hard, Lazarus stepped back and shuddered violently. "Did that mofo curse me?" He quickly made the sign of the cross, and as his hand went up it instinctively found his own wound. He noticed it for the first time. "He almost tore off my fucking ear! It's just hanging on!" Blood seeped through his tattooed fingers.

Buck took in a large gulp of air and exhaled loudly. "He's dead," he announced. Rolling Hans on his back, Buck's grubby fingers pried the shiv from Hans's neck and wiped the blood on Hans's boxer shorts, as if it was the most natural thing to do. "I'm going to retrace his steps while they are fresh, before it rains, and find that saw." Off Buck went following tracks that were entirely flat-footed, but he lost the trail once he entered the jungle.

Monty hoped the death of Hans would purify the air of any lingering malice and that the shared terror would be a bonding experience.

CHAPTER 26: The Burial

"You do it, son. You got skills. Just do it," Lazarus demanded.

Trent looked grim at the prospect of performing field surgery on Lazarus's wound. "I'm gonna try and stitch him up. Can you guys take care of that? It's going to start stinking." Trent gestured toward Hans's body, which flies had begun to buzz around anxiously, as if it was any old random roadkill. Against his inclinations, Trent took the newfound pot and started boiling water to cleanse Lazarus's ear wound and prepare it for stitches. "At least he's dead now, Laz," Trent said. "That was a good hit."

"Get his hands, would you?" Monty asked Rod, who looked at him beseechingly. "Go on."

Rod grabbed Hans's clammy hands by the wrists and Monty lugged his ankles. They set to dragging the cannibal's body along the shore and away from their camp, then deep into the jungle for burial. The effort to disguise what was done was instinctual. Rod kept scanning the sky for drones, not paying attention to the body. "There they are! Oh, this is all on video!" Rod shrilled.

"Of course it's all on video," Monty said. "I stood there like a bump on a log."

Monty recoiled and Rod's eyes filled with mute apology every time Hans's head hit something as they pulled him along. They both avoided looking at Hans's glassy unfocused eyes. Monty wasn't in the mood for talking. The body was heavy. When their arms got tired they simply stopped and dropped him. Monty knew he'd feel remorse after his shock wore off.

"Should we take them?"

"Sorry? Take what?" Monty asked in a daze. His eyes were stinging from the sweat he'd been unable to wipe away. He, too, was zoning out. He didn't want to focus on the gruesome task at hand. He couldn't think of what else there was to take from Hans.

"His clothes. He's big. That's a lot of material, cotton."

Monty sat back on his haunches and didn't respond for the longest time. "We might as well. Lord knows we may need them someday and I'd hate to dig him up later." Monty's imagination envisioned many gruesome scenarios and the smells likely to accompany them. They peeled the damp shorts off his body and wrangled Hans's trunk out of his blood-soaked top.

"Maybe he didn't know," Rod muttered, looking at the rolled-up shirt.

"Know what?" Monty asked.

"Maybe he didn't know the duffel bag he took was the only one dropped for all of us to share. Monty, I have to tell you. Hans came to me at night watch. I think he came and stood there watching and listening to us. It wasn't the first time. I told him to go away. I told him to leave us alone. He didn't say anything. And then when he came today I blinded him. It made him susceptible to attack. That was horrible."

"Don't tell the others that. It doesn't matter now, Rod. It's done. I've never seen someone die."

Rod sat back. "If that's your feeling maybe he was your first. Did you see Buck's face? I think...I think he liked it." Rod noticed everything. "We should say something, a word over Hans."

"Why in the world would we?"

"It's what it wants." Rod sounded odd.

"It? I'm not following your line of thinking, buddy."

"The island, the host."

Monty looked into Rod's eyes. "Rod, your eyes are dilated. I think you're hallucinating." Monty handed the clothes to Rod, who had a visceral reaction, dropping them like hot coals.

"What now?" Monty barked in frustration.

"I can't handle those. I can't touch them."

"Why not? You mentioned taking them, and you helped pull them off him just now. What the heck?"

"I don't know. Oh, Monty, I don't know." Rod began running his hands through his hair.

"Calm down," Monty said. "First things first; I'm closing his eyes." Gently, he eased Hans's eyelids down. They popped back open involuntarily. Rod shrieked.

"Dammit! Don't scare me. You're working yourself up." Monty set to digging with the tiny shovel as Rod slowly rocked back and forth to comfort himself.

Monty dug and discoursed. "Buck was right about one thing. This soil is shit. No sandy grave for the cannibal. I'm hitting volcanic rock. We can't bury Hans here. Maybe we should take him to the lagoon and let the sharks finish him off. Like he ate those girls."

They dragged a now-naked Hans to the lagoon. Strangely, a hoard of sharks was gathered, swimming erratically with their fins down.

Monty asked Rod about the oration. "What words do you want said? Words for the living or words for the dead?"

"I'll do it." Rod spoke slowly. "Hans Fritzl finished his lifetime here on Island X. We give him back to the earth. May he find forgiveness. May we also find forgiveness. And please, let this be the end of negativity on the island."

There was no dignity in Hans's disposal. On the count of three, and closing their eyes, Rod and Monty chucked him in with clumsy determination. He floated like a cork for a minute until the sharks, with their powerful jaws, set to rudely snapping, pulling, yanking, and wiggling, churning up the water with the carnage. The macabre savage feeding frenzy tossed spray in all directions. Hans was shredded in seconds. Monty threw up the curdled contents of his stomach, macaroons, adding more food to their feast. The sharks disappeared quickly, leaving nothing but a dark stain in the water.

Lurching back to camp with the sun setting behind them, Monty felt creeping fear and a humming in his ears. The full horror of the day's acts set upon him. His shadow seemed longer than normal and slightly out of step with his movements. He chalked up the phenomenon, the mental slippage, to adrenaline, hunger, and the insanity of the day.

Back at camp, he saw that Hans's blood in the sand had drawn hungry rats that were snuffling around, eager to desiccate its owner. Monty almost threw up again. He shooed them off and kicked sand over the blood.

CHAPTER 27: The Kill Video

"Someone stole my entire pack of K-Cups. This is the second time this has happened. Pisses me off no end," Bledsoe bitched. "I'm going to find out who did it."

Jessica Overstreet entered the room and clapped her hands together like a coach at a Little League game. "Okay. Hans the Cannibal. Since the operation has made headlines, the president is considering announcing his demise. His victims' families are still raising holy hell, banning together in shared disgust. I can't say that I blame them. I wouldn't be surprised if some Israeli faction was planning to drop a bomb on the island. Showing them the cannibal's demise should put an end to it."

"That footage was intense. Those sharks, the way they dispatched his corpse." Bledsoe gnawed his thumb, wanting to discuss the event.

Jessica issued crisp orders. "John, I need you to edit the video without sound. Show the cannibal confronting the others, his attack, the ear bite, the two men dragging him to the lagoon, and the shark disposal. Edit it with an eye to the chance *anyone* could see it."

"To whom will this be released, other than the president and the Israelis?" Bledsoe asked.

"To those who need to know, and when they need to know it, John. It doesn't play well to have the Israelis ticked off. Politics are strained enough. So, like I said, you, Branson, and O'Neill need to do a couple of edits for my selection. In this instance, the more it appears like karmic retribution the better," Jessica said. "Oh, and no close-ups of their faces while they're talking either. Remember, lip-readers." Jessica tapped her lips with two manicured fingers.

"I don't know how much more swift and sure of a karmic attack you can get," O'Neill remarked. "Someone might even say this was planned. Fritzl ate people and then sharks ate him. What if the other victims' families find out and demand the same?"

"Like who? The base attack by Cooper was pretty well hushed up. I'll give you that some guards would love to see Lubbuck put in a bag, smothered, and drowned," Jessica countered. "Anyway, get 'er done. Smooth sailing, boys," she chirped.

After she left the room, Branson said, "Just do what she asks, John. Why do you always question her?"

"Did you see her tailored power pantsuit? She'll stomp you in it. Actually, that would be amazing," O'Neill added.

CHAPTER 28: Anti-Curse Maneuver

Trent spent a good portion of the night ministering to Lazarus's torn ear. Upon hearing of Hans's burial at sea, Lazarus crabbed, "You should have brought back his head and we use it as a paperweight."

"Let's divvy up the rest of his stuff," Buck declared. "There's an MRE for each of us and we've inherited a damn bungalow. What do you call it—a timeshare?"

"There's no way I'm sleeping in that place," Trent stated superstitiously. "And I don't feel good about eating from a cannibal's pot. I didn't like using it to boil water. It's creepy."

Buck sniggered. "It's not like he cooked humans in it."

"It's good. It's Oggun," Lazarus said of the cauldron.

"Huh? What?" Trent asked.

"It filled with a Santerian spirit. Oggun," Lazarus declared. "He lives in the wilderness and is the god of the hunt."

Drained, the group partook in a long rest. By morning, up and jazzed, Lazarus announced his plan for exorcising any lingering evils. "I'm gonna call on the Heavens for some spells."

"Spells? Wait a minute. I thought you're Catholic," Monty said.

"Santeria is a version of Catholic. Our spirits are doubled up with the Catholic saints."

"But you were just banging on about the cannibal and black magic. How's spell casting different?"

"I know some white magic, protection spells. Good stuff. My Aunt TT used to do it. First, we see if there is bad juju in us. We'll have to make do with what's on the island. I'll improvise. Get fresh eggs from Birds' Nest. One for each of us."

Buck swatted away Lazarus's suggestion with a snort. "Count me out. I'm going to search again for that saw." He headed off in the direction of the cannibal's camp.

"Get four fresh eggs, son," Lazarus directed Trent. "While you get them, I need to make us a ritual bath to clear the negative forces."

Monty was intrigued by the process. Lazarus procured herbs from his knapsack and set Hans's water pot to boil. He steeped the plants for half an hour, saying prayers over them that none of the others could understand. He set the mixture aside to cool. When Trent returned with the eggs, Lazarus took an egg in hand.

He started with Rod. Lazarus began with supplications and incantations. He ran the egg along

Rod's body from head to toe, lightly skimming the shell along his skin. He made swiping and flicking motions with the egg. At the end of the gestures, he cracked it on a rock and examined its contents. "His looks good." While both Monty's and Rod's eggs were clear, Lazarus and Trent were not as fortunate. Their eggs had what looked like spots of blood in them. Even those who did not believe seemed to grow nervous.

"No good. We need two white birds now," Lazarus said gravely. "I won't hurt them," he told Rod when he visibly paled. Two white terns were captured. In almost the same manner as the eggs, Lazarus gently rubbed a live bird over Trent's body from head to toe and allowed it to fly away, squawking madly. He then did the same for himself. "The birds take away the evil."

"That one just crapped all over the place," Trent noted.

Lazarus said prayers over the herb-infused ritual bath. Lazarus instructed Trent to kneel and said prayers over him as well. Lazarus beseeched Mother Mary to participate and accept the sacrifice. He poured a bowl of cooling water over Trent's head. He did the same for himself.

"We all need head prayers, more protection now that we're clean. For all of us. We need four coconuts and four bowls of water."

A coconut was gathered for each man. Half of each was mashed, the other half ripped into four sections to be used for divination. One by one Lazarus faced each recipient and began speaking in a foreign tongue, saying words with lots of vowels. Using many quick gestures, he passed the bowl of mashed coconut over each man's neck, shoulders, hands, knees, and feet. He said, "Salt water make the evil go." Using a coconut filled with water, he dipped his fingers and made the sign of the cross on each man's forehead, nape of the neck, temples, throat, inner elbow, palms and feet. He applied the coconut mixture of mash and milk to the same blessed parts, except the head, and told each man to pray. He took the four sections of coconut and threw them behind each man and scrutinized the resulting pattern. He asked questions like, "Are you pleased with the offering?" Sometimes he threw the rinds and asked more questions. When the pattern flipped to two rinds with the whites up and two rinds with the brown sides up he looked relieved and finally stopped.

CHAPTER 29: Unmoored

Trent was the first to experience a breakdown. What started with his incessant scratching of bites had turned into a lingering malaise, and then feverish infection. The next afternoon he complained of cold and body aches. He flatly refused to leave the tent, as if his sanity was moored inside it.

"Where's Trent?" Monty asked Lazarus.

"Tent. No bueño. He upset. He needs to rest." Lazarus then whispered to Monty, "Maybe killing chomo was wrong. Maybe we are cursed now."

Monty sighed so long it seemed to exhale all the air from his lungs.

"At least that god-awful whistling has stopped," Buck remarked. Buck had taken to brazenly strutting around stark naked, subjecting the others to his bare ass.

"He was whistling 'cause he was happy," Lazarus said.

In the tent, Monty found Trent tossing around, half asleep and mumbling a name: Scotty.

Shaking him awake by his thinning shoulders, Monty asked, "What's going on? Who is Scotty?" He saw Trent had his false teeth removed and was babbling nonsense. "You are feverish." Monty brought him a plastic bottle of rainwater and Trent took a sip and spoke.

"I dreamed I was that lady that got killed in the bank I robbed. I was waiting in line to cash a check and draw out money for my son's soccer camp. And I was beating myself up about some Popeye's fried chicken he begged for and then only ate the skin. I saw this chubby kid in my mind as clear as day and I felt a great love. I was in that bank standing in line and this horrible man in a mask burst in and I was terrified. I couldn't breathe and I couldn't run. He made me lie on the ground. My face was to the floor and I kept thinking about Scotty and how I'd yelled at him about the chicken and his smelly gym socks. They were always turned inside out in the hamper. I was that woman. 'Who is going to take care of Scotty?' I never felt despair and fear like that. I felt what that poor woman went through. The teargas and gunfire. It was smoky and it stunk and stung. Then everything went black, a black that swallowed everything. Oh my God. What did I do to her?"

"It was just a nightmare," Monty stated without conviction.

"No, it wasn't. I've been having them all the time. I feel weird...attacked," he said, alarmed.

"By whom?" Monty was immediately on alert.

"The dreams. These bugs. This malevolent force. This island. We're its food, dude. It's gnawing on us ... physically...spiritually. We're reprieved corpses."

"Trent, is this about what happened with the cannibal? A delayed reaction? Or did Lazarus's curse chatter and spells rattle your cage? That performance was over the top."

"No, it wasn't any of that."

Monty attempted to rouse his spirits. "Listen, man, before we landed here our lives were forfeit. No more. This is our second chance. The prison now is only in your mind. Remember a time when you were innocent?"

"So many years ago. If you told me last year I'd be on an island I would have thought you were insane. But now, maybe this is our justice. I feel more mortal than when I was in a death row prison cell on SCU. We're in its world now. Fate is following its own course. And I'm scared."

"Don't confuse your imagination with reality. You're just sick and feverish. It'll pass. Take some Advil. Lie down, rest up, drink water, and quit fucking scratching."

Monty neglected to inform Trent about his own eerie dreams. Crawling out of the tent, Monty considered that Rod may be correct about the EMFs screwing with people's heads.

Meanwhile, Lazarus and Buck were in conversation about the island's hothouse environment.

"Seasons? There's only one season here, hot." Lazarus was talking about the harsh, unrelenting sun. "Maybe that's his problem too. The humidity is making it feel hotter."

"And the sickening trills of these goddamn birds, and rats everywhere," Buck added.

"Never thought I'd be sick of crabs and pescado," Lazarus said.

"I want meat." Buck licked his sun-blistered lips. "Red meat, not just bird flesh."

"I know. Just something different." Lazarus waxed nostalgic. "An old nutraloaf looks good right about now. Carbs. I would never have thought a nasty mash-up of bread, potatoes, carrots, cabbage, beans, and onions would sound like heaven."

"Good old vomit loaf," Buck added sarcastically. "I don't know if I'd go that far. I survived on that for quite a while. I was on nutraloaf for two weeks in solitary and they threw it at me like I was a dog. When I asked for something to read, those bastards only gave me cookbooks. If that's not torture I don't know what is. Imagine eating nutraloaf while reading about parmesan-crusted prime rib."

Monty thought of prime rib and began to salivate. "Rats are even starting to look good. Sorry, Lazarus, but I'm ready to try one. What diseases could they possibly have on this island? They run all over our stuff anyway. Let's try one."

"Rat jerky? No mas rata. Maybe we are gonna die of starvation."

Rod, who was looking less sharp-boned and more robust as the days passed, spoke animatedly. "No. No. You're all wrong! We are around so many living things to sustain us. The plants thrive. The rats aren't dead. Crabs aren't dead. The birds aren't dead. Neither the fish nor the sharks. We can live too. We can thrive too. Lazarus cleaned the energy field. The island is transformative. We can find a kind of happiness here if we learn how."

"It's too much work. I spend all day scrounging for food. We are marooned. Who else wants off this fucking island? We can do it. Make a raft, use a parachute as a sail, tack against the wind, and float the fuck away to wherever we want," Buck urged vehemently.

"Wait," Monty declared. "Hush with the cynical bullshit. Stop being the denizen of doom. You don't even know where we are. What you're suggesting is suicide. You'd have to fight against the tide just to clear the island. If you try to leave you put all of us in jeopardy. They will shoot you, and us too!"

"He's right," Lazarus agreed dejectedly.

Scenting drama, Rod said, "The earth offers humans all they need to survive. You all are mentally stuck in an artificial construct. Why would we want to go back to that?"

"Fuck this construct. I'm leaving," Buck whispered malevolently.

"If you so much as make a rowboat I'll mark you," Lazarus said.

"Buck's just t-t-tired," Rod blurted in excitement. "We're hot and t-tired. The EMFs are getting to us."

Whirling around, Buck yelled to the clouds in frustration. "What the fuck?" He pointed violently to Rod. "EMFs." He spat at Lazarus. "Chupacabras and spells." Buck flung his arms around, fiendishly raving. He pointed at the tent. "The same cursed whistling over and over!" Then he pointed at Monty. "This old dude's majestic, royal proclamations from on high. I am sick to death of looking at and listening to all of you!" He kicked the sand like a spoiled child. "I want off this island."

Lazarus shook his head at Buck. "Changueria. Hissy fit."

"Someone needs a t-t-time-out," Rod deadpanned bravely.

Monty and Lazarus burst into laughter until they were weak-kneed and holding each other up.

That's when Buck snapped, giving vent like a volcano of old, and seemed to take on the island itself. And like a volcanic eruption, the men stepped back and watched him go. First, Buck ran for a palm tree and punched the trunk repeatedly, shrieking and hollering. "Not Island X. Island Hex!"

He wants to kill or inflict pain on something, Monty thought.

Buck then dashed for the lagoon—a good ten-minute run—and splashed around, pounding the water and kicking at the looming sharks. More obscenities than can be written down issued from Buck's frothing mouth as spittle flew in all directions. He screamed at the black-tip sharks. "You hungry? Eat my ass!" Even the sharks had the pea-brained presence of mind to avoid him.

The culmination of his rant involved him running through Birds' Nest trying to snatch up something, but all wildlife slipped or flew away from his fevered grasp, except for the eggs he crushed underfoot and through his knuckles. Distressed birds wheeled overhead dropping shit all over him. Before an audience of rancorous creatures, Buck's rave ended with him in the fetal position blocking his ears and covered in egg yolk and bird guano. He was finally spent from punching away at life. He cried and cried.

That night, Buck did not return to the main camp, but instead slept in Hans's old structure.

CHAPTER 30: A View of the Stars

It was midnight when Monty dragged himself beside Rod. "Buck certainly ran amuck and went off the deep end. I can't say I've ever seen anything like that. It's like we're seeing the worst of ourselves exposed in each other. Breaking down."

"Did he come back yet?" Rod asked.

"No."

"Everyone breaks. Some just take longer to do it. His anger was his armor," Rod said.

They sat in silence until Rod said, "'Death will slay with wings whoever disturbs the peace of the pharaoh.'"

"I've heard that before. Where is that from?"

"It was on a tablet they supposedly found in King Tutankhamen's tomb, but it was allegedly destroyed. It's the curse of the pharaoh. It popped into my mind with Lazarus going on and on about curses. It's weird what pops into your mind. All I know is Egyptian curses and anything spiritually having to do with the Egyptians had like four layers of meaning."

"What are you saying? Are you implying there is something to this curse thing?"

"No, not necessarily," Rod said. "It's probably a natural occurrence, what's been going on with Trent. But have you noticed the birds are acting weird? They are staying low to the ground now and picking up on information fields. Everything is feeding. The clouds don't look right either. The island does not like environmental stress. Something's about to happen. Something is trying to get our attention. My brain feels deluged with information. Trent senses it too." Rod's beard was growing out and he pulled at his chin like a prophet heralding catastrophe. "I have a gut feeling. We will see," he stated sagely.

"Gut feeling bad or good?" Monty asked dispiritedly. "Never mind, I don't want to know."

"The greatest ideas and sensations have been coming to me. So many, both good and bad. I'm sifting through them. The electromagnetic fields are everywhere. I just keep thinking to myself, don't stick your foot in the water so deep that you can't pull it back out."

In the wee hours, when Monty gave in to fatigue and returned to his tent, Rod took a stick and began walking the shoreline. He paced a distance in the gray moonlight, bent over and began marking the sand, pushing the stick into its moistness, making symbols. Like everything else, his actions were captured by the drones and filmed.

"It is finished," he said to the eye of the sun when it rose.

CHAPTER 31: Analysis

Branson and O'Neill filled in Bledsoe with the dailies. "The good news is Rod started writing on the sly. The bad news is we're having a whale of a time with it."

"Why? We're supposed to be taking notes like STASI agents. Shouldn't the cameras capture every nuance?"

"Because, first, he's scribbling in the sand. Lots of lines and circles. Second, it's at night. Third, it's at high tide. The placement of the writing, with its temporal nature, means it's probably meant for us," O'Neill said.

"Save the individual screenshots to a file," Bledsoe directed. "We'll kick up the contrast and loop them together and send them over to the engineering department and let them take a crack at it. Oh, and crop Rod out of the frames. If you can't, then censor his face. Did either of you take calculus?"

"Nah. College Algebra," O'Neill laughed.

"We knew anything he wrote would mean nothing to us," Branson admitted.

Bledsoe squinted at the hundreds of screenshots. He tapped a monitor. "This...this is the big clue. This is fantastic! This means a promotion. A yacht. A house in Kauai."

It was not so fantastic.

"Well, the engineers are either highly amused or pissed. I vote for pissed," Branson declared. "Let me read you their reply.

> *Per your request, the subject writing was initially analyzed by our department but was largely unintelligible. The documents were then sent over to the computer science team for further analysis and it was determined that the writings were in binary code and roughly translated reads: Sometimes the only person who can see is a blind man.*
>
> *Is this your idea of a joke, guys?*

"Hot Rod. What a cheeky little asshole," Bledsoe said.

"It looks like you won't get that promotion yet," O'Neill quipped.

Branson mused aloud. "What is Hot Rod trying to say? That he's fucking with us?"

"He didn't seem the type," O'Neill observed.

"He sits out on that lava rock like a hermit. How can he stare at the sky so long without blinking? Tell you what, I'm gonna buzz his ass tonight with a drone," Bledsoe declared.

CHAPTER 32: The Wrath of Island X

Having taken a hard look at the island, no one was quite sure who the first victim was to truly taste her wrath, her misfortune, her blighting hand. Was it the shark's attack on Buck? Was it Hans with the shank embedded in his neck? Was it Trent with his infected bites? The island was full of lies and illusions. Baleful by her own design, while saturated with life she's also saturated with death, like ants on a freshly dead bird.

The same sun that kindled life also kindled death and madness. The moon, which pulled the tides, also pulled on their nervous systems. Each man had to conquer not only the outer jungle, but also his inner jungle. With her infectious madness, she exacted her own brand of revenge, according to their degree of responsibility. She was perhaps not paradise but the underworld.

CHAPTER 33: The Hurricane

Bledsoe lost the petty opportunity to buzz Rod. Rod's receptivity to nature was prophetic, because the next day a hurricane struck the island. The air was alive with static electricity. The sky turned black, a profound darkness. Then the wind howled. The trees bent sideways, some snapping off with great cracking and tearing sounds. The spitting rain turned into a lacerating monsoon. The surf attacked the shore and the sea whipped into a frenzy.

When the rain began, the men battened down in their tents as they normally did. But very soon their concern grew. "If I know anything, I know a hurricane," Monty yelled over the gathering noise.

"Good news. We'll have abundant water," Buck hollered from his tarp, which he had stationed between the two enclosures. The wind buffeted their tents, sucking the air in and out like an old man having an asthma attack, like a fireplace bellows.

The water rose. When the tide came in, they were forced to higher land, grabbing their belongings in a panic. Rod was ready with his things neatly packed and prepared, along with the hand shovel.

With tremendous force, the hurricane pounded and battened the island for an undetermined span of time. The men felt like it went on for days. The roofs and Lazarus's tarp were snatched away into the atmosphere. Mighty torrents of rain and wind slapped their faces as they crouched in the underbrush. Any time they lifted their heads the wind bit their cheeks.

"Grab the pot and lie on your stuff!" Struggling to stay anchored to land, they clung to it like fleas on a dog. "Remain completely flat!" someone yelled. Lazarus began muttering nonstop in Spanish and begging an entity named Chango to stop the storm. Monty gritted his teeth and willed the nightmare to end.

Trent, shaken by his fever, was still weak. He yelled to Lazarus, "Oh my god! They knew a storm was coming and deliberately dropped us here."

Rod smiled. "This will down some drones. I will use the solar cells to make something."

The eye of the hurricane lingered off the shore of the island. While it watched from that vantage point, the men were powerless as insects under a microscope. The only might each could claim was his own ability to cling to the earth.

CHAPTER 34: Bad News

"A hurricane hit the island last night," Branson informed Bledsoe the minute he entered the room.

"How many casualties?" Bledsoe inquired.

"No idea. The drones are acting up, both the audio and video—frankly everything. It's some kind of spooky anomaly. Many are probably downed in the water."

"That's not supposed to happen. What's going on? Why do we have to use these insider contractors for everything? So-and-so's brother or uncle with crapola products who bill us millions of dollars."

"What's strange is that *all* of the electronics are non-functioning. Not just those made by Warburton. Even the monitor for the microchips is showing nothing but static where they were showing the microchips floating in the ocean."

"Why weren't we notified about an impending storm?"

"I don't know. The National Weather Service said it seemed to form from out of nowhere. 'Act of God.' O'Neill went to meet with them. There's not much to see now. All the static is creepy. I've been sitting here reading *The Tommyknockers*. Don't read Stephen King when electronics go haywire."

CHAPTER 35: Providence

After the storm ceased, Monty rolled in his tarp and collapsed in exhaustion. A few hours later he jolted awake when Lazarus popped under Monty's tarp. "Monty! Yo, those castaways, did they lose their heads?"

Monty's eyes focused on Lazarus's ear, still wrapped in a bandage crafted from his du-rag. "Huh?" Monty blinked slowly to clear his vision.

"Your story. That *Albatross* crew who made it to the shore and died. Were they beheaded?"

"I just got to sleep, Laz. I'm exhausted. I don't know. Why?"

"I was searching for my tarp and Trent's grill. I saw something, something malo. A ghost chica walking and holding her freakin' head, mayn! I'm cursed!"

"What? Where? It's probably a downed tree with a dangling coconut. What do you mean holding her head?"

"Like a freakin' soccer ball. Wearing an old-timey dress. Holding her head like a freakin' ball. Oh Jesus and Mother Mary, save me. I'm cursed!"

"Show me where."

"Oh no no no no no," Lazarus moaned in a strangled tone.

Monty saw that Lazarus's hands were shaking. *Vida loca, indeed*, he thought.

"Maybe someone set sail here to hide from the law and you saw it wrong. Maybe you got a fever and delirium from your wound. Maybe it was a mirage. Witnesses never see things right. Or maybe we're losing touch with reality, a collective craziness. None of us got enough sleep. I can assure you there is no chica out there wandering around. Lie down under here." Monty slipped his tarp around Lazarus. "I'll go check it out."

Monty went alone, but armed. The story was so crazy he knew it couldn't be true. *It's nerves. It's just nerves. Go look,* he told himself. His own raw energy fertilized his imagination.

Monty took the walk slowly to clear his head, trying to shake a deep impression that something indeed was wrong. First, it was deadly quiet and somber. *Jesus, the storm came and wiped shit out.* On the path he found the shoe Rod lost the first day.

The sodden and mushy landscape had been altered by many downed trees, leaving a vast, desolate feeling of impermanence. He saw something odd in the distance, an apparition in the lagoon. More than the usual amount of water had gone out to sea at low tide. His heart flipped and flopped in his chest. There was something in the amorphous contour of a woman. With an animal-like sense of danger, every limb hair on his body was standing to attention.

In a dreamlike state, Monty staggered toward the motionless figure. A weird creeping mist, fitting his mood, blanketed the lagoon. The shape loomed awkwardly. Monty strained his eyes, squinting to them to slits, and shuffling forward. At twenty feet the object came into focus. Stupefied, Monty approached the lagoon's shore and entered the water, wading out toward it.

It was easily six feet tall. Its rear was indistinct, covered by barnacles and seaweed moss. Circling it slowly, its visage was serene. It did have a head on its shoulders, unlike Lazarus's recollection. The bowsprit was perhaps the oddest and most unique one Monty had ever seen, and obviously carved by a master craftsman. A long-dressed woman proudly held the head of a man in the crook of her left arm.

"Fuck me sideways," Monty muttered.

Her face was beautiful and victorious. A captor who had claimed the ultimate spoils. How long had she lain submerged in the lagoon? How many decades? The force of the storm must have righted and uncovered her from her watery grave. Relief washed over Monty's body. It's just a figurehead from an old ship, maybe one of the two vessels stuck here so long ago, he reassured himself. Monty reached up and placed his hand upon her breast. It was cold and slick. The dark oak wood was fossilized. The figure's face was unweathered and likely preserved by the lagoon's floor. *Lazarus and the others will have to come and see this for themselves.* Monty had to admit how downright uncanny it was that the blocky figure managed to stand herself. Maybe the government was messing with them after all. He collected his wits on the walk back.

When he returned, Monty saw Lazarus, with Monty's blanket draped around his shoulders, had been lured out from under the tarp and sat huddled fraternally around the unlit fire with Trent, Rod, and Buck. Despite his weakness, Trent was attempting to start a fire. The others watched dispiritedly. Rod had also discovered using glasses did not work on this island to start a fire.

"You're never going to believe what I found. I see your confusion though," Monty said to Lazarus.

Lazarus's eyes were popping with alarm.

"Did you find my teeth?" Trent asked.

"No, I didn't find your fucking teeth. I did find Rod's shoe." He tossed the shoe, which Rod caught single-handed. Monty refused to reveal the secret to which he was leading them. With laggard steps, they followed him to the lagoon.

"I promise you, you're going to laugh," Monty insisted with a rueful smile.

"If you are messin' with me, I'm marking you next." Lazarus was jangly and in a foul mood, grumbling along. Then the substantial fog that was mantling the lagoon magically parted and lifted the veil from his eyes. It was like a rainbow appeared. "Oh dios mio! Madre di Dio!" Lazarus dashed out to the shoreline. "Mary! It's the Holy Mother! Yemaya! We prayed for the curse to lift and you came!" He gestured wildly to her in supplication. "She here! She came!" Lazarus splashed out to her in abandon. "Mother of Oceans! Mother of the Fishes! Yemaya."

"What the—? What the devil is it?" Buck said aloud in bemusement. "Does he think he conjured it up?"

"Maybe it's part of a silly fucking game," Trent said dispiritedly.

The bowsprit, facing the sea, seemed to guard the lagoon. She was positioned so that she appeared to float upon the water.

"I wonder what else is in there," Buck said. "Maybe there's parts of a boat in there."

The auspicious presence of the bowsprit seemed to becalm the men. Lazarus spent the morning in ritual, wading out to her in worship, pantomiming like a priest, wreathing her in flowers, and festooning her with libations, seafood, and shells in multiples of seven, placed on floating palmettos that looked like fans.

"What are you doing?" Trent asked him.

"Giving back to the Mother. She is here. She has ashé, energy. Can't you feel it?"

"You are starting to sound like Rod," Trent said. "A less romantic conclusion is that it's a piece of wood."

Lazarus said, "I'm a romantic. Don't be so grouchy."

CHAPTER 36: Confusion

Bledsoe had the office to himself.

"Here. Finally," he exclaimed in relief at the resumption in communications with the island. Bledsoe had been working a Sudoku puzzle Branson left behind but had not made much progress. His eyes scanned the various monitors for active drones. "Let's see. What are our little criminals up to today?" he said to himself. "Talk to Daddy."

A drone stationed at the lagoon picked up what appeared to be the presence of six figures. Bledsoe shook his head in confusion, clicked the zoom button, and pushed up the volume.

"Oh, Madre di dios! Mother of Oceans. She came!" Lazarus was kissing the bottom of some large trunk-like object. "Yemaya!"

"What is that? What the hell is a yemaya?" Bledsoe's thumb instinctively went up to his mouth and he began gnawing.

By the time Branson came back from lunch Bledsoe had chewed all his nails to the quick, ripped the healing skin around them back in strips, and was spinning his empty coffee cup in confused circles.

"Bob, shut the door. Shut the door," he cautioned.

"What's up? I brought fresh bear claws." The grease bled through the paper bag he held aloft.

"This is what's up." Bledsoe reversed the video. "What's going on?"

Branson sat silent for a few minutes, chewing slowly, polishing off a glazed claw. Bledsoe clicked his pen to annoy him. Branson finally said, "What newspapers covered that area in the 1800s?"

Bledsoe blinked dumbly at him in irritation.

Branson continued after swallowing. "There was at least one shipwreck there. It looks like an old ship's maidenhead. The way I recall the story a ship caught up on coral and never made it into the channel. So I have no idea how the figurehead got there, but if the ship made it into the lagoon that would explain it. It was probably concealed and stirred up by the storm. Just get the old news reports."

"What department would that be, Bob? Seriously, could this get any weirder?"

Branson raised his chin at Bledsoe's cup of coffee. "What number you on, John?"

"Don't start. I have to stay awake somehow watching these screens. I can't sit here stuffing my face. And they are out there...out there...screwing around." Bledsoe sputtered for words.

"Don't get spun up. Calm down. It's a piece of wood. It's a carved tree trunk. Find out what country the *Albatross* sailed from—wasn't that its name? That should be a good starting point. The island has a tragic history, but don't most places? Chill out."

Bledsoe reached for the bag of bear claws. "But how did it get there? And what other treasures or relics might be in that lagoon? This isn't good. So help me if this is another joke. I still have egg on my face after the Rod fiasco—binary code. You or O'Neill are telling Equal Op Overstreet about this. I refuse to do it." Bledsoe stuffed his mouth. "I refuse."

The object left them scratching their heads as they consumed all the pastries. They decided O'Neill would tell Jessica.

CHAPTER 37: Absolution and Desecration

The bowsprit garnered a lot of attention in the days that followed. The statue buoyed Lazarus's spirits. He waded out to her like a religious procession declaring, "She bring us good fortune." He confessed a good deal of his previous misdeeds and shortcomings to her, all of which were collected via surveillance and noted to the file.

Buck and Monty were fishing on the shore together, dragging the shallows with a mosquito net. "Look at Laz out there kowtowing like a fool," Buck said under his breath.

"What difference does it make? There is no harm in it. It makes him happy," Monty replied.

"It's probably some goddamn Trojan horse and he treats it like a Catholic confessional. Too bad Rod can't swim."

"Like Rod has anything on his conscience. The bowsprit is like a mother figure to Lazarus. Everyone loves a mother."

"Not everyone," Buck spat. "I was adopted. I found my real mother, my vagina mother. I found her. She married some rich dude. Turns out she wanted to be with this guy and a snotnose kid was not part of the package. I went to surprise her on my birthday. No heads-up. Nothing. When I knocked on the door no one would answer. There was a Lexus and a Hummer in the driveway, and I could see lights on. After a minute I hammered my fists. An old man answered and I asked for her under her maiden name. I could tell he was suspicious. Once she came to the door she looked me up and down, in the eyes— same color as mine. I said, 'Hi, Mom. It's my birthday.' She paused a second then denied me. She said, 'I don't know who you are. Don't come here again.' How's that for a mother? Happy fucking birthday."

"That's a shitty story," Monty agreed.

Lazarus, with his daily offerings and supplications, was not the only man interested in the bowsprit. Monty thought he'd seen it all when, that afternoon, he spotted Buck desecrating the statue. Or making love to it. Or some version of both.

At night watch, he detailed Buck's amorous exploits to Rod. Without fanfare or preliminaries, Monty said flatly, "I saw Buck screwing the bowsprit."

"What? But how?"

"Don't ask. But he was…talking to it too. I think it added juice, no pun intended, to his fantasy."

Rod recoiled. "She's like the island's Great Mother. Oh, you can't tell Laz! You cannot. Because you know how Laz feels about her. He reveres her like she's divine. He'll mark Buck and make him fair game."

"When is Buck going to stop acting like a delinquent teenager debasing everything? He prides himself on being difficult, juvenile, and hedonistic. Lazarus could have easily happened upon him instead of me. Why does he do this shit?"

"I get the feeling the island wants...to be obeyed," Rod murmured.

"Obeyed? Are you oracling out on me again? Let me see your pupils."

"He pulled in negativity by doing that – a vortex in an energetic sea. That was bad." Rod's pupils were as wide as an owl's. "Bad. Bad. Bad."

"Stop. You are reminding me of that craggy-faced character who doles out warnings in horror movies."

"Bad." Then Rod lapsed into silence.

CHAPTER 38: A Curious Specimen

Bledsoe read aloud from an article dated 1865 printed in the *Daily Dramatic Chronicle*, an early version of the *San Francisco Chronicle*.

> *In sailing news, on an unfortunately named vessel called the Albatross, traveling from California bound for Jarvis Island, thirteen souls lost their lives. The ship was sighted by the Valkyria lodged less than one mile off the coast of a small atoll. Valkyria's crew boarded the vessel and, upon inspection, a fair amount of provisions were still on board. But no men on deck. The captain's log was retrieved. No distress flag was raised on the nearby atoll. The Albatross was transporting mined guano from Jarvis Island.*

Branson blinked. "Okay. So?"

"A ship sailing to pick up guano isn't going to have a figurehead like that. It just wouldn't," Bledsoe insisted.

"Maybe the figure was from the *Valkyria*. What else is on file? I'm sure this is explainable."

"No, I found a picture of the *Valkyria*. I tried to find information on other wrecks. In 1904 a Japanese vessel got hung up on the coral too. They were poaching feathers to sell for French hats. That boat wouldn't have a fancy figurehead either. We can't go to Equal Op Overstreet with some sort of half-baked folkloric explanations, Bob. We need records, charts, data…facts."

"Where is the captain's log now? I mean, what do you think we can discover one hundred and fifty years later? It's not like they had criminologists and coroners going out there to investigate a shipwreck a thousand miles away."

"The marine research center in San Francisco houses relics. Wanna make a trip?" Bledsoe suggested. "Or we can carbon date the bowsprit."

"I thought about that but we'd have to have someone land there and take a sample. Let's not sound the alarm," Branson said. "It's too risky. And it will expose the fact that somehow, in some way, we did not do our due diligence here in choosing this atoll."

Instead, they took a set of high-definition images of the figure to an expert on ancient cultures and maritime history at The Smithsonian.

"It's a curious specimen indeed." The expert raised his glasses to look the agents. "Where did you say it is located?"

"We didn't," Bledsoe replied.

"If someone told you this is Victorian they miscalculated. Is it hollow? This artifact is in an amazing state of preservation, but I'm not sure it is in fact a bowsprit, as you suggest. First, it's not angled like a typical bowsprit. I don't see anything that would attach it to a boat. Second, see this side? This almost looks like a seam, which would be more apparent if not for the barnacles due to it being in the water."

"What is it then?"

"Fellows, I believe this object is a wooden sarcophagus. If you seek a second opinion, try a funerary expert."

CHAPTER 39: Mother Mary

No one had to tell Lazarus anything. The lei of flowers around the figure was missing. In addition, the evidence of Buck's pleasure was on the face of Mary's headless victim. Lazarus, holding his arms out and away from his body as bodybuilders do, approached Buck.

"You fucked Mary!" Lazarus's words were like a bullwhip through the air.

"Huh?" Buck affected indifference, but his backtracking movement betrayed his truth.

"Someone needs to WD-40 your ass because you ain't slick." Lazarus leveled a finger at Buck and howled in anger. "You put your nasty penis on the Holy Mother!"

"Don't get all salty. The opportunity presented itself. She was open for business." Cocksure, Buck mocked Lazarus's upset. Stupidly, Buck had sped past the danger point.

"You touched something sacred. Defiler!" Lazarus eyes were slits.

Buck was unhumbled. "They put it here 'cause they are playing with us. Can't you see? Don't worship it. It's a hunk of wood, not a fucking shrine!"

Monty cut his eyes at Trent. Before anyone could react, Trent emerged from behind and struck a blow to Buck's head with a walking stick. Buck buckled over, knocked unconscious.

Lazarus and Trent trussed Buck's hands and feet with parachute straps and floated him out into the water. They had planned their attack. They tethered him to the bowsprit up to his shoulders in the lagoon.

Buck regained consciousness and twisted uncomfortably. "Come on, guys! Be reasonable. You're not gonna hurt me over this," Buck wheedled. "I can't stand up. I'll drown out here when the tide comes back in. Or the sharks will eat me."

Monty knew that once Lazarus rashly got his teeth into something he would not let it go. Monty spoke evenly. "Come high tide Buck will be submerged. He shouldn't die this way. No amount of tropical sun can bleach out the sins we've already done. We can isolate him."

"He wanna be with her? Let him!" Lazarus shouted. "Let him sleep with the fishes tonight."

Buck changed tack. "Listen, Laz, I'm not playing games. I saw her and for a moment she wasn't just a statue. It's like she came to life and was talking to me."

"What she say?" Lazarus asked skeptically.

"That's true. He was talking to it," Monty said, trying to appease Lazarus.

"Listen, she said she was here because you called her and that I could tell her anything. And she said she would provide whatever comfort I needed, spiritual or otherwise."

"Liar! You're a dirty chomo liar!"

Buck began screaming for Monty and Rod and God, none of who appeared to be listening. "I'm sorry. What do you want, a human sacrifice? Untie me. Don't let him do this!"

But Lazarus had hardened like the wood of the figure. So Buck, just like he did at his criminal trial, decided to unsettle them.

"Don't you miss female companionship? She's the closest thing we got," Buck said. "C'mon, Trent, let me loose," Buck begged. "You don't have to do everything Lazarus says." When Trent pointedly ignored him, Buck changed tack and doubled-down. He flung his next words like a whip. "You're nothing but an ass kisser. Have your balls even dropped yet? You let Lazarus call you son. You make yourself subject to him. He's a sociopath."

"And you're an asshole," Trent responded.

Buck, spitting spite, yelled at Trent. "Fuck you, you toothless buzzard."

"Teeth or no teeth, I'll live longer than you."

The last image Monty had was of Buck crying out in distress. "Help me! Please, somebody help me!" He was flailing against the straps that fettered him.

Lazarus instructed Rod to take watch over Buck and the bowsprit.

CHAPTER 40: In the Light

All was quiet right before dawn. Monty had fallen asleep on the lava rock. He lit a torch, walked to the lagoon, and waded out to the bowsprit. What he saw struck fear into his heart. The parachute straps still wrapped around the trunk were neatly snipped in half. In spite of the dawning heat, Monty was chilled to the marrow. Where was Buck? Who set him free? Monty took the straps.

"What did you do with Buck?" he queried Lazarus, who arrived with his arms laden with the morning offerings. Trent lagged behind.

"What you mean? Where's asshole?"

"That's what I'm asking you," Monty said in frustration. "He's gone and the straps are cut. See?" Monty showed him the ends. "You don't have him?"

Lazarus splashed out to examine the area while Trent stood on the shore rubbing his forehead in confusion.

"Where's Rod?" Trent asked.

"He was sleeping when I got up," Monty answered. "So if y'all didn't let Buck go, and Rod and I didn't let him go, how'd he get free? These straps appear to be cut. Not frayed. Not chewed. Not ripped. Cut."

Lazarus gnawed his upper lip. "Where that saw?"

"The cannibal's saw? We never saw it. Buck said he never found it," Monty said.

"Aye mio. You believe what Buck said?"

"But he couldn't have the saw because he was naked as the day he was born when we tied him up. Remember?" Trent said to Lazarus.

"I'm going to ask Rod." Monty headed for their tent and shook Rod awake. "Buddy, where's Buck?"

Rod blinked hard and rolled his eyes. "Trussed up like a pig last I saw."

"Well, not anymore. He's vanished."

"He's free? Good. It wasn't right trying him up like that." Rod lay his head back down on a T-shirt stuffed with feathers.

"No. Not good. Not good at all, in fact. Get up."

Rod roused himself and followed Monty to the fire.

Lazarus and Trent were in deep whispered discussion as Lazarus was pacing around. "You know, maybe you both freed him." He pointed an accusing finger at Monty and then Rod.

"I can assure you I did no such thing," Monty insisted. "Nor do I have a cutting implement to do so.

And Rod can't swim so he hardly swam out to let Buck loose."

"You were supposed to watch him," Lazarus yelled at Rod.

"I got t-tired," Rod whined. "It was h-high tide. I refuse to watch someone d-d-drown. The water was up to his neck when I left."

"Laz, listen. Maybe Buck had the saw hidden on him," Trent suggested. "The tip. Maybe he found Hans's saw, lied about it, and was secreting the tip on himself just in case. Or maybe the cannibal had the saw on him when he was killed and they took it!" Trent pointed at Monty and Rod.

"Again, ridiculous," Monty insisted. "This whole thing is nuts. You prayed and this thing appeared. Hell, maybe she freed him. Now we've got another boogeyman to deal with."

"This is shit. Bullshit! She did not free him. Maybe there was a seashell or something sharp in the water he used. But she did not free him."

"The lagoon, it swallowed up the evil." Rod shuddered. "Or maybe it was a Mil-Ab. The government carried him off. Those whirlybirds are silent and can be here and gone and we'd be none the wiser. That's the simplest explanation. It was a military abduction."

"Rod's right. Maybe Buck was a spook," Trent suggested.

"No, he's real," Lazarus argued. "You going loony too?"

"No, a spook is an undercover CIA operative," Trent said. "An intel op."

"Why do you say that?" Lazarus questioned.

"Remember that first day we landed and how he was questioning and quizzing all of us? He was digging for information like he was CIA. FBI. NSA. DOD. Something."

"Fuck that alphabet shit!" Lazarus declared.

"Why did they have Navy SEALs drop us here?" Trent said. "Think about it."

"Mil-Ab. Mil-Ab," Rod chanted.

"Just about the time we could relax, get settled, and spread out that jerk goes missing. All of y'all are stirred up. Now we'll be shadowboxing again," Monty complained. "I am not in the mood to argue with you guys. I did not free him and he's gone. I'm taking a walk."

After the initial shock, Buck's disappearance effectively killed conversation around the island.

CHAPTER 41: COME BACK

Agent O'Neill was the man on the wall, assigned to watch the screens during Bledsoe's and Branson's absence. While they were meeting with the antiquities expert they received a simultaneous text reading: *Return ASAP. Lubbuck AWOL!* Accompanied by an angry emoji.

Branson knew better than to put sensitive information in a text. "Greenhorn," he muttered. He and Bledsoe departed immediately for headquarters. Jessica was alerted and had already worked up a head of steam.

"It's not possible. Tell me it's a mistake," Jessica insisted. "What do you mean we lost our mole?" she yelled about Buck's disappearing act.

"Don't worry. Buck will home back to camp like a pigeon," Branson stated.

"He was put there on the island to be the irritant, the grain of sand in their oysters that created little pearls of wisdom. Where could he have gone? Who did it? What do the other inmates know?"

"He's the last person on that island they'd think to be cooperating with us," Bledsoe insisted. "Buck did try to escape from the SCU, remember? So this isn't against his nature to pull a Houdini. He's probably hiding."

"Has anyone watched the monitors? Viewed the footage?"

"Yes, but there was a glitch," O'Neill said. "The footage glitched."

"A what?" Jessica snapped. She looked like she wanted to shake O'Neill like an English nanny. "Is Lubbuck still there or not? Find out now! Security on the island was supposed to be easy to maintain. That's why it was chosen. Constant surveillance and no interference. Someone get the recon men on the line. Now! Nobody goes home until this is figured out. And Rod better not be harmed because he may initiate dead man triggers." The men waited until Jessica left to speak again.

"Dead man triggers? What?" Branson said.

Bledsoe threw this pen across the table. "There goes my promotion. We're useless. I don't even know who stole my fucking K-Cups."

CHAPTER 42: Revelation

"I need help dragging some heavy lava rocks," Rod said to Monty when he returned.

"What for?"

"You'll see. It's a surprise. When I find ones I like I'll come and get you, okay? We'll put them on a tarp and pull them." They began gathering them and dragged the rocks one by one to the lagoon until there was a sizeable pile. Monty was satisfied to put his mind on labor.

"I need to roll these into the water," Rod said.

"Oh, you're going to make a little tide pool. Smart."

Rod waded out gently into the lagoon after Monty assured him the water level was only waist-high in that area. "The water is safe here," Rod mumbled repeatedly to himself for assurance. He eased himself in like an old man into a warm bath. He began placing the heavy rocks in a crescent shape, attempting to create a small dam. "Come here. Stick your head under."

"What for?" Monty whispered warily, pulling back. "You drowned Buck, didn't you? Oh my god! You put him out here and you need me to help you weigh his body down?"

"No, nothing like that. Don't be afraid. I was once offered something. Go under." Both Rod and Monty submerged. "Presidential pardon!" Rod screamed under the water, then put a finger to his lips.

They came up and looked at each other. They took a breath and went back under. Rod repeated it twice.

"Why?" Monty yelled.

"Anti-gravity spaceship," Rod garbled. It took four attempts for Monty to understand.

"How?"

"Plasma. Antimatter. Propulsion technology. EMFs."

None of this made sense to Monty. The only thing he understood was that there was a bigger plan afoot the entire time. Rod jumped out of the water and had a panic attack on the shore.

Later, once Monty talked Rod down, he confided in him. "You asked me about my family's politics. One time my uncle got sauced and maudlin. I hated when he acted like that. It was the anniversary of my parents' accident, and Uncle Bobby said that maybe his politics played a role in their deaths. My father was helping him with his memoirs at the time of my parents' car crash. My dad was taking it to an attorney to have it vetted."

"What happened to the manuscript?"

"It was burned in the accident. It was just a typewritten draft. Uncle Bobby got drunk and, I'll never forget, he said, 'Maybe it was for the best,' which I thought was a messed up thing to say."

CHAPTER 43: Clandestine

"No Man is an Island."

Jessica Overstreet called an emergency meeting. "I have been informed Shane Lubbuck was pulled."

Branson cocked his head.

"Pulled? What do you mean by pulled?" Bledsoe asked.

"It looks like we are not the only covert operation in town," she replied crossly. "It was kicked upstairs, sent up line, or sideways. NSA. CIA. DARPA. Some group on a black project."

"Oh please. Just shoot me," Bledsoe said.

"I can't. I already shot myself," Jessica snapped, leaving the room in a huff. She slammed the door but they could hear the click-click of her heels down the hallway.

"It was a Mil-Ab. It was the No Such Agency. They were looking over our shoulders the whole time," Bledsoe said. "Renegades operating outside laws and government. I bet they were messing with our communications too."

Branson laughed. "The left hand doesn't know what the right hand is doing. Each organization is an island unto itself, no pun intended."

"Island X. Fuck this compartmentalized bullshit. We were all plowing the same ground," Bledsoe stated.

CHAPTER 44: Flight of the Mole

The powers that be were intensely watching the mole. Once Buck was attacked and tied up by Lazarus and Trent, they sent a helicopter speeding toward the island. It reached Buck in the nick of time.

He stunk, literally and figuratively. They didn't care for his welfare. They didn't clean him up, so that he wouldn't look like he'd been gone if they decided to return him. That was still up in the air.

Buck felt immense relief and surprise when the chopper lifted him into the night sky and away from the island. The air inside crackled with intensity as the hatch slid closed.

"Who are you," Buck asked. His question was ignored.

"That place is hell. I don't want to be there any—"

"Air him out."

Buck's commentary was cut short when he was gagged, grabbed by his ankles and dangled outside of the craft as it flew along. He crapped himself, which blew away in the wind. He was hauled back inside. "You have not held up your end of the bargain."

A dark-suited older man got down to business. "You have two choices: go back to the island and get

Roderick Cooper to talk, or I'll push you out right here. The drop may hurt you, but we'll suit you with a life jacket so if you survive the fall you'll float along until you are too exhausted to move. You can swim in any direction and never hit land. Becoming more tired, thirsty, and hungry as the days go by, with little sea creatures nibbling your toes. I was in the Navy. Floated nearly two days. You've never known real fear until you are treading water in the dark, not knowing up from down or what's underneath. What's your decision?"

"There isn't one. Take me back. But give me something to eat," Buck said. He was handed a piece of beef jerky, which he consumed like a ravenous dog.

Buck was debriefed, rebriefed, chipped with a cyanide-filled capsule under his triceps muscle and dropped back on the island. "Redeem this mission. The fun and games are over." He was placed in the dead of night on the opposite side of the island, back by the cannibal's hut.

CHAPTER 45: The Voucher

The sky was an odd orange-red and the clouds hung around the sun like wet mummy wrapping. Something about the bowsprit had been bothering Monty. A line. He swam out and ran his fingers along its surface. There it was—a seam. He began picking at the barnacles around it until his knuckles were bloody. In Monty's peripheral vision he detected movement from shore.

"Something is odd about that thing," Buck said, as if he had not been gone. "I noticed that while I was tied up to it."

"Look what the rat dragged in. How did you get free?" Monty asked.

"Had my shiv. The higher the water got, the more slack in the lines," Buck lied. "Those fuckers almost killed me."

"What do you want, Buck?"

"Truthfully, I don't want to die today. I'm not good at apologies."

"Where have you been?"

"Hiding in a rotten log for two days. I'm starving, man. You got anything to eat?"

"No. I take it you want to accompany me back to camp to talk to the others?"

"Has Lazarus calmed down? Listen, you don't have to advocate for me. Just please don't advocate against me."

"Stay here. I'll go talk to them," Monty said.

"Thanks, man."

∞

Monty did not understand what compelled him to advocate for Buck. "Hey guys, don't freak out," Monty announced. "Buck is at the lagoon."

Lazarus's immediate reaction to Buck's reemergence was tucking a weapon in his pants.

"I think we should let him come back," Monty told them as they made their way to the lagoon.

Lazarus stopped short and poked a finger to Monty's chest. "Whoa. You vouch for this asshole? After all you said about him?"

"The island spared him," Rod agreed. "It's not like he did anything to us."

"Disrespect. If you vouch for him and he does anything, you're done too," Lazarus informed Monty menacingly.

"That is pitting me against you. I won't do it," Monty insisted.

"I will," Rod trilled. "I vouch for Buck."

Lazarus snarled. "Buck is on his own. You on your own then, too."

CHAPTER 46: The Royal Scam

"They who enter this sacred tomb shall swiftly be visited by wings of death."

King Tut's Curse

The twenty-minute walk wasn't enough time for Lazarus to calm down. Sensing danger, Rod literally ran ahead of Lazarus.

"Our fate is intertwined now," Rod said to Buck. "You can stay, but you have to be good."

"Glad to see you are all being reasonable. And I'm happy we're all here because I have something to say. An announcement, if you will." Buck took a deep breath. "Listen, Rod, if you don't tell them what you know, we'll all be bombed."

"What *I* know? What do you m-mean?" Rod replied, totally taken aback.

"There's not a lot of time for us here, Rod. You know the information the government wants. Give it to them and we can live safe and unharmed," Buck said. "Save us."

Monty angled himself between Rod and Buck.

"What this asshole talking about?" Lazarus asked. No one responded.

"What did Monty tell you? Why did you tell him, Monty?" The betrayal in Rod's eyes was palpable, his eyes welling with tears.

"I did not tell him anything," Monty said, turning to face Rod.

"But you and I, we were underwater and—"

"I did not tell this jerk anything!" Monty insisted, slapping his hands together repeatedly for emphasis.

"Well then, who did?" Rod paused and then pointed at the reddening sky. "Ah, *they* did. *They* put him here."

"Yeah, so?" Buck said, confirming Rod's suspicion.

"They put you here to squeeze information out of me? Their last squeeze?"

"Yeah, so?" Buck repeated.

"You're a spook!" Trent exclaimed.

Lazarus paced, flicking his fingers.

"Do you know what you're asking? Which entity are you working with? Do you even *know*?" Rod screamed. He stepped backward toward the lagoon.

"I don't care. I know that if you don't give them what they want they plan to blow this island sky high. All our deaths will be your fault. Like those men you blew up in the government building. It'll be your fault!"

"No no no no no no," Rod sputtered. "They'll throw a few sacrifices into the volcano before they figure out it doesn't work. What they don't know is that there is consciousness beyond them. They are not morally advanced enough to handle the information."

"Stop with the nonsense gibber jabber. If you want us to stay conscious today then play along. Do you see the drones? They are aimed right at us," Buck said, pointing here and there. "Start writing. They said it was a formula that would fit on an index card. They gave me a notebook and some pencils to give you."

"The numbers, they are all wave forms," Rod shrilled. "Ones. Zeros. Ones. Zeros. I wrote on the beach to give them a clue. Everything is equations."

Lazarus yelled at Buck. "You idiot. You think they gonna just let us live after he gives up the goods? That's snitchin'. You know what happens to snitches?"

Trent attempted to sucker punch Buck with his stick but Buck ducked and dodged. Trent's swing made him lose his balance, hitting Monty's skull with a thunk and breaking the stick in two. While Trent was off-balance, Buck seized him, placed him in a headlock and dug a broken bottle into his throat. Stepping back, a kangaroo punch away from an unconscious Monty, Buck addressed Lazarus. "You want to see what happens to snitches? I'll demonstrate. Back off." The shard pressed against Trent's jugular.

Rod issued a scream that seemed to emanate from the ground, fueled by volcanic energy. In terror, Rod began wading out to the bowsprit.

CHAPTER 47: Resumed Communication

All hell was breaking loose at the Washington headquarters. "Wait. Look, guys. Is that Buck?" O'Neill said while zooming in with a drone.

"Yep. Kick up the volume."

"Where's that motherfucker been?" Bledsoe wondered aloud.

"We'll find out," Branson said. They reacted to the situation enfolding on the screens.

"So he's been on the island the whole time? Rotten log, my ass."

Jessica entered the war room looking worse for wear. "Buck's back. This entity thinks they are so much more competent than we are. As far as I'm concerned he's their problem now. Let them manage this op. I don't want any Benghazi shit on me. Fuck this."

"So are they taking over or are *you* making this decision?" Bledsoe asked. "And are you saying we are to take no action? Buck has reappeared and is talking to Monty. We could be getting somewhere."

Jessica's phone buzzed. "Stand down. I have to take this call." Jessica left without further explanation.

Branson, Bledsoe, and O'Neill remained mesmerized by the monitors. Bledsoe was hot. He couldn't recall ever being so angry. He watched Lazarus, led by a running Rod, march to the lagoon. Bledsoe felt helpless and that helplessness fueled the anger.

"Buck's gonna get answers. Or, maybe not," Branson stated.

"Buck's got no finesse," O'Neill noted. "Always the bull in a china shop."

"Again with the stick, Trent, you used that move already," O'Neill chided at Trent's wild swing, which struck Monty, felling him like a tree. "Oh!" O'Neill choked.

"There goes Monty. That split the branch in half. He ain't moving," Branson said. "There goes one of the good guys."

"He's just knocked out," O'Neill remarked. "Oh, get up."

"This is all going sideways. Let's save this op," Bledsoe said, guiding a drone in closer to the men.

"Jessica said to stand down." Branson moved his hand to stop Bledsoe's.

Bledsoe pulled back with agitation. "Screw Jessica," he declared, baring his teeth like an upset Chihuahua.

CHAPTER 48: Island X

"What you gonna do, homie," Lazarus asked Buck, bouncing on the balls of his feet.

"Back up, Lazarus. We need Rod to tell them or we're done. This entire exercise is a covert operation to get some scientific information out of this genius, so let's get Rod and make him—"

Lazarus didn't hesitate. He was not going to take orders from Buck. He hurled himself at Buck and Trent in tandem. A drone, ready for strike and aimed at Lazarus, hit Trent instead. The drone moved in closer after its first strike. Lazarus and Buck tumbled around in the sand in a ball of violence. In the melee, another drone took aim and both Buck and Lazarus fell dead. The nearby birds took off in droves. Others attacked the drones and the agents saw beaks and feathers in their viewfinders.

Rod clung to the bowsprit, circling around it as if to hide himself from the helicopter he spotted coming closer. The black craft starkly set against the scarlet sky scared him. His fingers clawed at what appeared to be a hinge and, as if by magic, it cracked open to reveal a hollow coffin-like core. Rod scrabbled inside. "Oh no, oh no," he muttered.

The helicopter landed on the shore and men armed to the teeth in swat-type uniforms swarmed the lagoon. One man yelled, "Roderick Cooper. Come with us now. Your friends are down."

"M-Monty too?" Rod hollered from the sarcophagus.

A man put his gloved hand to Monty's neck and felt for a pulse. "Davenport's alive."

"Leave Monty here and I'll come with you," Rod yelled, poking his head out. "Do we have a deal?"

"Affirmative. Yes."

As Rod inhaled deeply in the musty sarcophagus, an immediate sense of calm pervaded his body.

"I want to you to say it. On camera. And I'll come out. That if he's still alive you'll leave Montgomery Davenport here unharmed. Leave him a first-aid kit. Only then will I come with you and tell you what you want to know." Rod closed the bowsprit.

"Affirmative. We'll leave Davenport here unharmed." He addressed a man inside the chopper. "George, toss out a first-aid kit."

The men waded out to Rod and escorted him into the helicopter. It lifted into the air as the sky began to slowly darken.

∞

"Buck's got what looks like a bottle shard to Trent's neck. Oh geez. Look at Lazarus. He's bowing up."

"Should we take a shot at Lazarus? Aim the drone right at him," Branson asked.

"I'm doing it." Bledsoe sited the tattooed man and triggered the drone to hit him.

"Dude. You just hit Trent," said O'Neill.

"No, I didn't." Bledsoe's hand was shaking from adrenaline.

"You better hope Rod lives."

"Where's Rod going? Oh shit. He's going into the water. He's going to drown himself. Scramble a chopper to—" O'Neill yelled.

"What's that? A Black Hawk? Copycats! They are probably going to take out Lazarus. Screw this. I'm hitting him first. Engage!" Bledsoe, having already made one mistake, was eager to salvage the debacle. He took aim at Lazarus, triggered the device, and both Lazarus and Buck slumped to the ground. No one knew whose equipment did the damage. Did the deathblow come from the Black Hawk? All they knew is that Buck and Lazarus ceased rolling and froze in a dark comical embrace.

"At least Cooper is still alive and he's crawled in that...thing. That sarcophagus."

"It's a sarcophagus?" O'Neill appeared surprised. "Like to put a dead body inside?"

"We didn't have time to update you because we got your text about Buck going missing."

"So, who put a coffin—"

"Shh! They've got Cooper. Where are they going? Track the radar. Set a drone to follow those fuckers."

"On it. Flying due north." Branson's drone followed the Black Hawk.

"Heading to?"

"Tracking via radar north. I'm guessing Hawaii."

Bledsoe commandeered another drone and followed along.

"Where's Jessica? Rod must be talking. Yes! Yes!" Bledsoe raised his arms in the air like his team scored a touchdown.

"Hold up. The craft is descending. It is going down. What's going on?"

"That isn't right. They are over water. There must be some kind of malfunction. There are no ships nearby. They are going straight down."

"Oh my God," O'Neill squealed.

As the men watched, they would later swear time seemed to slow. They were helpless to assist.

"It's gone," Branson said. "The chopper hit the water at over one hundred miles per hour. It's in pieces."

"There's a leg. Oh, I can't..." O'Neill turned away from the monitors. "Turn it off."

"We can't."

They circled the craft with the drones and watched the bits and bobs sink into the Pacific, and then it was nightfall.

Jessica entered the room. It filled with a lingering silence.

"What did they find out? What the hell happened?" Bledsoe yelled at her. He put his hand on her shoulders and shook her until her hair came out of its bun. Branson pried Bledsoe off their superior and corralled him on the far side of the room.

Jessica took a few minutes to rearrange her hair and nerves. "The information was not retrieved. It was a total abject failure. We're all being reassigned. Someone will be in to speak with all of us. This did not happen." She pointed at each man in turn.

"But, I hit... I activated..." Bledsoe sputtered.

"This did not happen. The inmates placed on the island killed each other. That is the story. And if you so much as lay a finger on me again I'll put a bullet between your eyes," she hissed, breaking her composure.

"What about Montgomery Davenport?" O'Neill was shaken.

"I don't know. I just don't know. He may not even survive." She looked at a blank space on the wall for a full minute. "I drank your K-Cups, John."

"You can't just leave Davenport out there wounded," O'Neill insisted.

"Pack up," she declared.

∞

Two men in suits and sunglasses arrived to talk to the agents. The security documents were arranged in fat stacks for each agent to sign. Many generic statements. They were told to sign their full signature and social security number to each page at the bottom.

"Sunglasses, really? You're inside the SCIF," Bledsoe snarked.

"What about Montgomery Davenport? Is he even alive?" O'Neill asked.

"Sometimes watching targets makes an agent have feelings for the target. Get over it," one of the men in sunglasses replied.

Branson was frustrated. "Did you put that sarcophagus out there?" he beseeched the other man.

"That is no longer your business, but no, we did not."

"I feel demoralized," O'Neill complained under his breath. "Like the men of Island X."

Bledsoe muttered to O'Neill and was rebuked. "You were read into this project and now you're out. Don't forget... you're disposable."

"Do we get to read these?" Branson asked, gesturing to all the papers.

"You'll get a copy later. You are never to discuss this assignment."

Later never came.

CHAPTER 49: Above Island X

"…all is in little." Alexandre Dumas

Rod was handed a pencil and a notebook. As the equation spilled onto the page, an agent noticed Rod sniffling. "Don't be upset. You made the right decision. It's over once you finish. We can put you back on the island to enjoy the remainder of your life."

Rod sniffed again. A drop of blood from his nose stained the paper. He wiped his face and saw blood smearing the back of his hand.

"Oh. The universe always leaves itself an out." Rod managed a wry smile.

"Was this man hit?" the agent said to the others.

"No, no sir. He probably has a nosebleed from the altitude."

"Death will slay with wings…" was Rod's final statement. His eyes rolled back into his head and the blood began pouring from his nose.

"What's wrong with him? Keep him alive. He's not finished," said a man in business attire who was watching over Rod's shoulder.

The last mark on the paper trailed to the bottom right corner, decorated with blood spatter.

An agent bagged the contents while another attempted resuscitation on Rod.

Rod lay limp as a rag doll. As the agent performed chest compressions he noticed something wet on his hands. Blood from his own nose.

The ancient bacterial spore Rod had deeply inhaled in the sarcophagus worked quickly through his body, and through those in the aircraft. A sketchy radio transmission roughly detailed the unfolding incident. A few miles away from Island X the pilot lost consciousness and the chopper plummeted downward into the ocean.

No one has disclosed the true nature of what occurred—until now.

The next morning Monty woke up on the beach with a lump on his head the size of a bird's egg. The sun was burning his face but a slight breeze lifted his hair, playing with it. He rolled over. There was carnage. Trent. Buck and Lazarus with their blood comingled in the sand. Eventually, Monty dragged the bloated bodies out to sea. Rod was gone. Monty had no memory of what had happened. He found a first aid kit nearby. He also discovered a pad of paper and a pencil next to a tree at the lagoon, on which he wrote this story.

Out on the lava rock at night, Monty talked to Rod and felt an amazing energy radiate back. "I feel it now, buddy." In his fantasies, Rod had escaped the island.

The government sent no more prisoners to Island X. Monty grew old on the island, alone.

As the years passed, he noticed the drones less and less.

Proof

Made in the USA
Columbia, SC
02 July 2017